MOURNING DOVES

MOURNING DOVES

stories

JUDY TROY

CHARLES SCRIBNER'S SONS · NEW YORK
Maxwell Macmillan Canada
Toronto
Maxwell Macmillan International
New York   Oxford   Singapore   Sydney

Eight stories in this collection—"Mourning Doves," "Birthday," "In One Place," "The Nevada School of Acting," "Geometry," "Looking for Love," "Things to Care For," and "Secrets"—originally appeared in The New Yorker. "Famous People in History" appeared originally in Icarus (Number 5: Winter, 1992). "Prisoners of Love" first appeared in Antaeus (Number 70: Spring, 1993).

Charles Scribner's Sons   Maxwell Macmillan Canada, Inc.
Macmillan Publishing Company   1200 Eglinton Avenue East
866 Third Avenue   Suite 200
New York, NY 10022   Don Mills, Ontario M3C 3N1

Macmillan Publishing Company is part of the Maxwell Communication Group of Companies.

Library of Congress Cataloging-in-Publication Data
Troy, Judy, 1951–   .
        Mourning doves : stories / Judy Troy.
             p.   cm.
        ISBN 0-684-19369-8
        I. Title.
PS3570.R68M68   1993   92-40933
813'.54—dc20

10 9 8 7 6 5 4 3 2 1

Printed in the United States of America

FOR MARY D. KIERSTEAD,

MY FAMILY,

AND IN MEMORY OF MY FATHER

Contents

The
Florida
Stories

The Way Things Will Be

On our way to Florida in the winter of 1965, Eddie, the older of my two brothers, had an appendicitis attack and was operated on in a hospital in Nashville. My parents didn't have much money—we were moving from South Bend, Indiana, to Key West, where my aunt and uncle owned a motel. My father's idea was for us to live in one of the units while he and my uncle started a fishing business. My father had been a car salesman in South Bend, and before that he had worked in a dairy, and before that he had sold suits in a department store. He said that people he worked for didn't like him. He said that he was the kind of person who should have his own business, because he was independent-minded and good at making decisions. My mother said she thought it took a lot of money to start a business of your own, but my father said no, it just took courage and intelligence, and a family that was willing to stand behind you.

In Nashville, while Eddie was being operated on, my other brother, Lee, and I slept on couches in the lobby. We had been up all night in the car. Eddie had been crying, and my parents had been arguing about what to do. My father had wanted to wait until morning to see if Eddie felt better, and my mother wanted to find a hospital immediately. In the middle of the night, as they were shouting at one another, my father took his hand off the steering wheel and slapped her. There was suddenly silence. As far as my brothers and I knew, my father had never hit her before, and he seemed as shocked as anyone. As soon as he could, he stopped at a gas station and got out of the car. He walked to the edge of the pavement, which bordered a field. His shoulders were hunched over, and he was looking down at his feet. He was standing just outside the circle of light that separated the gas station from the darkness.

My mother got out of the car, too. "If it weren't for Eddie I wouldn't get back in," she said, loudly enough for him to hear. "I'd find a bus and go back to South Bend." Lee started to cry. He was seven, and Eddie was ten, and I was twelve. My mother got in the back seat with us, and after a few minutes my father came over to the car and put his hands on the hood, as though he didn't want the car ever to move again. My mother told him to drive to a hospital.

After Eddie's operation was over, my father drove Lee and me to a motel on the outskirts of the city, because it was cheaper, and he gave us money to buy hamburgers at a restaurant next door. He said that he would be back before too long. "I'm putting you in charge, Jean," he said. "Take care of Lee." I made Lee take a bath, and I took a bath, and I unpacked clean clothes for us. It was raining, and we ran to the restaurant, which was a diner on a road that ran parallel to the highway. It was noon, and the restaurant was crowded with truckers. I ate my hamburger quickly and wrapped up Lee's to take with us. He had brought a toy car with him, and instead of eating his lunch he pushed the car back and forth across the table, crashing it into the sugar bowl.

At the motel, Lee fell asleep and I lay down next to him and imagined shapes of faces in the patterns that the streaks of rain were making on the window. There wasn't a TV in the room, and most of our books and games were in the car. There wasn't even a clock, and I couldn't tell how much time was going by until it began to get dark outside, late in the afternoon, and then I became really frightened. Lee was up by then, and he kept asking me when our parents were coming back. He didn't cry, but when I put my arms around him I could feel him shaking. I tried to make my voice sound normal. I invented games for us to play and after it stopped raining we stood outside, even though it was cold, so that we could watch for the headlights of our parents' car as it turned in to the motel. When our parents finally came, I was so relieved that I didn't feel angry until later, when I was in bed, trying to fall asleep. I thought about how scared I'd been all afternoon, and how happy I'd acted to see them, and I felt as though I'd been tricked.

They weren't speaking to one another—at least my mother wasn't speaking to my father. It seemed that he hadn't shown up at the hospital for a long time after he'd left us; he had stopped for a beer and got into a conversation with someone. My father liked talking to strangers. That morning, just before he'd driven Lee and me to the motel, he'd had a conversation with a nurse in the hospital lobby. "She thought we lived here in Nashville," he said cheerfully on the way to the motel, which made the motel seem even shabbier and lonelier than it was when we pulled up in front.

My mother sat on one of the beds with me and Lee. She told us what Eddie had said after he woke up, and what his roommate was like, and what she had eaten at the hospital cafeteria. My father was unpacking his clothes, but all of his attention was focused on her. Even when he wasn't looking at her I felt that he was listening unusually hard, that he was waiting for her to say something especially meant for him. She didn't, though. She sent him out to bring us back some dinner, and later slept in bed with me.

In the morning, my parents took us to the hospital with them—they didn't have enough money to stay in the motel again. We brought our Monopoly game in with us and set it up on a table in the lobby. My father was in charge of the bank. Each time Lee or I asked for anything he would say, "I'm not sure. What have you done to deserve it?" He tried to joke this way once with my mother and she took the money out of his hand without saying a word. After that we played the game as seriously as if the outcome of it would change our lives. I hadn't wanted to go to Florida to begin with, but now I felt as though I would do anything to get there, so that we could at least stay in one place. I started to think, This is the way things will be from now on— nothing planned.

After lunch, my father took Lee and me for a walk. We passed a pawnshop and a liquor store and a big vacant lot. It was winter weather, but warm compared to South Bend. The wind was pushing dry leaves and scraps of paper down the street, and dark clouds were flying across the sky. We could hear thunder in the distance. "Are we going to live here?" Lee asked. He was holding my father's hand.

"We're going to live in Florida," my father said. "You'll see the ocean every day, and it will always be warm outside. It will never snow."

"Why not?" Lee asked.

"Because it's too far south," my father told him. "It's where the birds in Indiana fly to in the winter."

He bought us ice-cream bars at a candy store and we walked back to the hospital. When my mother saw us, the expression on her face changed from serious to happy. My father put his arm around her and she didn't pull away, and we sat down on a couch in the lobby. They discussed what we were going to do. Eddie had to stay in the hospital three more days, and if we stayed in a motel again we wouldn't have enough money to get to Florida, and my parents didn't know how they were going to pay the hospital bill. My father didn't seem worried now that my mother had stopped being angry with him. "I think you should call your dad," he said to her. "He can wire us money, and when things are going well for us in Florida we can pay him back."

My mother said no at first, but changed her mind. As a result, later that afternoon we checked into a nicer motel—with TV. It was in downtown Nashville, across the street from a park. We ate dinner in the coffee shop,

and afterward my parents decided to go to the motel
bar, which had a band and dancing. My mother pushed
back the curtains in our room and showed us where it
was—in front of the motel, just across the parking lot.
It was a small, low building with red lights around the
windows and a flashing neon sign. "Dad and I will sit
next to the window and keep an eye on you, so you
don't have to worry," my mother said. "And if you
need us for any reason, just come out and get us. But
watch out for cars."

"Okay," we said. Lee was watching TV, but when
our parents left he went to the window and watched
them walk across the parking lot and disappear into the
bar. "We could go over there now and ask them to come
back," I told him. He shook his head; his eyes were on
the TV again.

At nine o'clock we both got ready for bed and I
made Lee lie down. I turned out the light and went into
the bathroom and sat on the floor to read *Black Beauty*.
I had probably read it twenty times before. I was reading
the part where Black Beauty is made to gallop with one
shoe missing when I heard my parents' voices. I went
outside in my nightgown. The stormy weather had
ended, and now it was colder and there was a bright
moon. Because my mind was still on my book, I was
feeling waves of pity for both Black Beauty and myself.
I had been crying, and my mother noticed the tears on
my face. "I'm sorry we didn't come back sooner,
honey," she said. She gave my father an angry look and
walked me inside. My father hesitated in the doorway.
Just in front of where he was standing the door to the
bathroom was open, and the light was on. He picked

up *Black Beauty* without looking at it and put it on top of a luggage rack in the open closet.

"Go back over to the bar if you want," my mother told him.

"Why should I?" he said. He closed the door. "Why should I do something I don't want to do?"

My mother helped me into bed, next to Lee. "I was reading a sad part of *Black Beauty*," I told her. "That's why I was crying."

"We're back now," my mother said. "Go to sleep. Everything's fine." I closed my eyes and listened to my parents undressing.

"May," my father whispered a little later.

"I don't want to talk now," my mother whispered back. I opened my eyes and saw that they were lying just at the edges of the bed, as far apart as if I had been lying in the middle between them.

"May, just put your arms around me," I heard my father say. After a few minutes my mother moved closer to him. "Things will be better when we get to Florida," my father whispered.

"You're always looking on the bright side," my mother said.

The next morning, my father took Lee and me to the park while my mother slept; we had woken up early. It was cold outside, and there were high white clouds drifting across the sky. We had Eddie's football with us, which we passed around—my father to Lee to me to my father. About every five minutes Lee would try to tackle one of us. We were the only people in the park.

But gradually more traffic appeared in the streets and buses began delivering people to work. My father seemed depressed all of a sudden. "Let's get Mom," he said. We walked across the street to the motel.

My mother was already awake and dressed. "I was watching you from here," she said. "I was spying on you."

We all went out to the car; we were going to have breakfast at the hospital cafeteria. "We have a flat," my mother said. She was standing next to the front passenger door, looking at the tire. She squatted down in her high heels and touched it.

My father came around the car. He rested his hand on my mother's shoulder. "We have nothing but bad luck," he said. "We don't have a spare."

My mother stood up. "How can you tell me something like that now?" she said.

"Can't we buy a tire or get it fixed?" I asked. Neither of them paid attention to me. They were looking at each other. They were having a conversation without words. I took Lee's hand and walked across the parking lot, and then across the street to the park. I was careful and crossed at the light, but I knew my parents would be nervous watching us cross a street this busy. By the time they called us back, though, we were halfway across. "It's okay," I told Lee. "They won't be mad at us."

We sat on a bench in the sun. After a few minutes, Lee got up to look at something shiny in the grass which turned out to be a dime. I watched my parents standing next to the car, arguing. I wasn't afraid that my father would hit my mother. I didn't think that would happen again unless, as in a "Twilight Zone" episode, we had to relive that night in the car all over again, just as it took place the first time. But I could see now that my parents were not going to be any happier in Florida.

I called to Lee, and he looked up at me. "Come over here and sit still for five minutes," I told him.

By this time, our parents were crossing the street. But they got caught in the middle of a yellow light and were stranded together on the concrete strip that separated the lanes of traffic. From where we were sitting we could hardly see the concrete strip—just their heads, which looked as small as flowers, above a steady stream of cars. "They shouldn't be standing there," Lee said.

"They'll be all right," I told him. The light changed, and they crossed the street without looking at anything except us.

Famous People in
History

My family—my parents and my two brothers and I—
spent January of 1966 in Jacksonville, Florida, living in
an apartment above a bar called the Starlight Lounge.
The lounge had dancers, and each night except Sunday,
as my brothers and I fell asleep, we listened to "The
Stripper." It was played at nine-thirty. "It's better than
a clock," my father said. "More reliable." He and my
mother stayed up later, filling and stamping envelopes,
which was a part-time job my mother had found. My
father was working as a janitor in a grade school. What
he wanted to do was start a fishing business in Key West
with my uncle, who lived there. That was where we
had been going when my brother Eddie had the appendicitis attack in Nashville. He had to go into the hospital
again, in Jacksonville, for an infection, and my parents
didn't have any money left by then.

Eddie was in the hospital for two weeks, and then he had to stay in bed for a week. As soon as he was well enough to go out, we drove down to the beach after dinner. As we were leaving our apartment, the girls who danced at the Starlight Lounge were coming in to work. They had big blond hairdos and wore short skirts and high heels. I had just turned thirteen, and I wanted to be like them when I got older, especially because my mother made unflattering comments about them. My father always said, "They probably have babies at home to take care of."

While we were walking along the water that night, my father said he was going to tell us a secret. "Getting stuck in Jacksonville was the best thing that could have happened to us. Now we know how bad things can get," he said. "We know we can get by."

"How do we know that?" Eddie asked.

"We're getting by, aren't we?" my father said. "We just had a delicious meal." We had had hot dogs and beans. "Now we're at the beach, all together as a family."

"I think what Eddie means," my mother said, "is how do we know things won't get worse?"

"Because I'm washing floors for a living," he told us. He walked off across the sand, toward the parking lot. Eddie and Lee and I started to follow him.

"No," my mother said. "Let's leave Dad alone for a while." She took Lee's hand and stooped down and began building a sand castle with him. He was seven.

"I was just asking a question," Eddie said. "I was wondering what would happen if I got sick again."

"Nobody's getting sick," my mother said.

"How do you know?" Eddie asked. "People don't know things like that before they happen."

My mother was looking up at the parking lot. It was getting dark, and the lights had come on. "Can you see Dad, Jean?" she asked me.

"I can see our car," I told her, "but I don't think he's in it."

We walked up to find him. Lee ran ahead of us, calling Dad's name, and he found him lying down in the back seat of the car. "I'm tired," my father told us. "I was resting. I worked hard all day." He was holding our map of Florida, which had the road to Key West traced in red ink—he had done that the night before we left South Bend. "It looks like a long way, doesn't it?" he had said. "But we'll be there before you know it, once we get started."

We got in the car, and my father drove through Jacksonville. "Why is there so much traffic?" he said. We were stopped at a red light. It was a Friday night, and there were teenagers in all the cars around us. Some of them didn't look much older than I was. It seemed like a long time since I had been around people my own age. My father didn't think it made sense to enroll us in school until we got to Key West.

"I know what it means to see teenagers out on their own like this," my mother said, pointing to the car next to us. "It probably means they're going to get into trouble."

"Maybe they just want to have fun with their friends," I said.

"We have fun," my father told me. In the back seat, next to me, Lee was rolling one of the windows up and down. "Quit that before I make you walk home," my father yelled at him.

When we got back to the apartment, we played a game my father had made up called Famous People in History. "I'm thinking of a president of the United States," he said, "who would be a professional basketball player today."

"Abraham Lincoln," Eddie guessed.

"I'm thinking of a president who would go to a dentist now," Lee said.

"George Washington," we all said. We were sitting in our small living room, which was also my bedroom. We could feel the *thump, thump, thump* of the music below us, and Lee stood up and did an imitation of a dancer moving her hips back and forth.

"Stop that," my mother said. She looked at my father. "How did he know how to do that, Edward?"

"How should I know?" my father said. He had imitated the dancers for us one day when my mother was out grocery shopping. What interested me more than the way they danced was what they wore, which still remained a secret. I had heard my mother once say, "Tassels," with disgust, but I didn't know exactly what that meant. The word came into my mind even when I wasn't thinking about the dancers. It came into my mind so often that I was afraid I would say it in the middle of an ordinary sentence.

"Let's listen to our own music," my mother said. She turned on the radio, and we listened to a song about a woman who was cheating on her husband, and then got hit by a train.

"That was a sad song," Eddie said. "Whoever wrote that must have really been feeling bad."

My mother turned off the radio, and she and I went into the kitchen and made hot chocolate. She stirred the pan of milk, and I looked out the window. There were two men in cowboy hats walking into the Starlight Lounge. I pointed them out to her. "Those men are regulars," I said.

"If we were home," my mother told me, "you'd be with your friends right now, at a slumber party or something, instead of watching men walk into a bar, or thinking about women dancing on a stage."

"They have a stage?" I asked. "I thought they just danced around the room, between the tables. But a stage makes more sense."

My mother poured the hot chocolate into cups, which we carried into the living room. My father was sitting on the couch, with his arm around Lee. He moved over to make room for my mother, but she sat in the armchair, instead. "I think we should find another place to live," she told him. "I don't care how soon we leave for Key West. I want to leave this apartment."

"What do you mean?" he said. "It's nice and clean here, and it doesn't cost much."

"You know what I'm talking about," my mother told him.

"Let's ask the kids what they think," my father said. He looked at us. "Does it bother you to live here?" he asked. "Do you think it's bad for you?"

"I like it," Eddie said. My mother got up and went into the bedroom. She came back out a few minutes later, when "The Stripper" began to play downstairs, and she made Lee and my father get up so that she could open the sofa. She got out the sheets and blankets and made the bed for me. After my parents went into the kitchen, I lay in the dark and watched the reflection of the neon Starlight sign flash in the windows of the building across the street.

In the middle of the night, when I woke up to go to the bathroom, my parents were having a loud argument. Eddie and Lee had woken up and were standing in the small hallway between their room and my parents' room. "What do you think we should do?" Eddie asked me. We were nervous because of the time on our trip, in the car, when my father had slapped my mother.

"Lee, go back to bed," I said. It was cold in the apartment, and he was wearing short-sleeved pajamas.

"I don't want to be in there by myself," he said. "I want Mom."

Eddie knocked on the door. He tried the doorknob, which was locked, and then we heard something break. I shouted for my mother to open the door. My father opened it a few seconds later. He had on a pair of boxer shorts, and my mother was standing behind him in her white nightgown. "Put on your bathrobe, Edward," she said.

My father put on his robe. "I dropped a glass," he said. "That's what you heard breaking." He showed us the glass, which was on the floor, next to the bed. Eddie and I started to pick up the broken pieces. "Leave those," my father told us. "You'll cut yourselves." He went into the kitchen to get a dustpan.

"I'm sorry we woke you up," my mother told us. "We stayed up late, talking. When people get tired, they get short-tempered. Then Dad accidentally dropped the glass."

"We were afraid Dad was going to hit you again," Lee said.

"That wasn't like Dad," she told us. "I don't think that will ever happen again. You should try to forget it."

My father came back in and cleaned up the broken glass. It was three o'clock in the morning, and it had started to storm outside. "Thank you for cleaning that up," my mother told my father, as though she were talking to someone she hardly knew.

"You're welcome," he said. Eddie and Lee went back to their bedroom, and I went back to my bed in the living room. The only sound in the apartment was the rain and wind outside. I woke up for a minute, just when it was getting light, and saw my mother sitting alone in the kitchen, with her back to me.

In the morning, my parents made breakfast for us, and then they went back to bed and slept until noon. Eddie and Lee were in the living room, fighting over the Etch-A-Sketch. "Both of you be quiet and go to your room," my father said, when he came out of the bedroom with my mother. They were still in their robes. He handed the Etch-A-Sketch to me. "Jean gets to use it," he said.

"I don't want to use it," I told him. "I'm too old for it."

"You don't look so old to me," my mother said. After a few minutes, she and my father went back into their room to get dressed. It was still raining, and I put on my raincoat and went downstairs and outside. I stood in the small covered entranceway to the bar, and one of the dancers opened the door from the inside. She was startled to see me. She was wearing a black leotard, black tights, and red high heels. Her blond hair was long and frizzed.

"Do you want something?" she asked.

"I live upstairs," I told her. "I was just standing here to be out of the rain." Behind her, I could see other dancers, up on a stage, rehearsing. The music was on, but not nearly as loud as it was at night. There were two men and a woman sitting at a table, drinking from coffee mugs.

"I can't let you in," she said. "It's against the rules."

"I shouldn't come in, anyway," I told her.

"I don't know how you fall asleep at night," she said. "I couldn't. I like quiet when I sleep."

"I like music," I told her.

"Janelle," one of the men at the table called out.

"Just a minute," she said. "I'm checking the weather. I don't like being in here without windows," she told me. "If it's raining or something, I like to know."

"I know what you mean," I said.

"How old are you?" she asked me. But before I could answer, the man who had called her name walked over. He was thin, and had large eyes and an old-looking face. He didn't seem interested in who I was or why I was there.

"Janelle, they're waiting for you, honey," he said. She said good-bye to me and closed the door.

I went back up to our apartment. My mother was in the kitchen, making lunch. "Don't ever leave like that again, without saying anything," she told me. "Especially in a neighborhood like this."

I sat at the table with my brothers. "We were hoping you got kidnapped," Eddie said.

"That's always been my wish for you," I told him.

"That's not something to joke about," my mother said. "A man tried to kidnap me once, when I was

19

thirteen. He pulled up next to me in his car and said, 'You have to come with me right now. It's an emergency.' "

"Why didn't you ever tell us that before?" I asked.

"I thought for two seconds about doing what he ordered," my mother said, ignoring my question. "Then I came to my senses and ran away from his car. This is why I'm always telling the three of you, 'Stay away from people you don't know. Don't trust strangers.' " She cleared the breakfast dishes off the table while Eddie and Lee and I watched.

"What would he have done to you?" Eddie asked.

"I don't know," my mother said. "I'm glad I was smart enough to run away. That's the important part."

Eddie and Lee went into the living room, where my father was sitting on the floor with their Erector Set, building a skyscraper for them. I was still in the kitchen. I didn't believe my mother had told the truth. I thought she had made up that story to punish me for leaving, but I wasn't sure, because it wasn't like my mother to lie. "I wouldn't scare my children with a story like that, even if it were true," I said.

"I bet you would," my mother told me. "I bet you would do anything to keep your children safe."

"This is not what I think of as Florida weather," my father said, during lunch. The wind was blowing tree branches against the side of the building. The bright overhead light was on, and the kitchen windows were steamed up from the pot of water my mother had boiled for spaghetti.

"The sun can't shine all the time," my mother said.

"How long are we going to live here?" Lee asked. He hadn't eaten anything, and now, for no reason, he burst into tears.

"Just one more week, Lee," my father said. "I promise." He got up from the table and walked around the kitchen. "Okay," he said. "Famous person, Lee. A man who had a lot of travel experience, but still wound up in the wrong place."

"Who would he be today?" Eddie asked.

"I don't know," my father said. "Never mind. Forget it." He sat down and looked at his coffee cup.

Lee got up and leaned against his chair. "It's Christopher Columbus, Dad," he said.

After my mother and I washed the dishes, we opened the sofa and sat on my bed with my father and my brothers, playing cards. My mother got up twice to look out the window at the weather. "Stop being so restless," my father said. He had told all of us earlier that we would be staying in the apartment until we left for Key West, and so now, when my mother got up and went into the bedroom, I was afraid she might come out carrying a suitcase. But what she came out with was a sweater for Lee.

"It's almost time for the Starlight Lounge to open," I said. "The first song will probably be 'Heartbreak Hotel.'"

"I don't think so," Eddie said. "I think it will be 'Take It All the Way Off.'" We listened carefully when the music started. It was a song we had never heard before, and whenever they played something new, they played it over and over again. By the time we went to bed, I thought, we would know it by heart.

Secrets

My father died in 1966, from a fall at a construction site where he was working, in Jacksonville, Florida. I was thirteen, and my brothers, Eddie and Lee, were eleven and eight. We had just moved from an apartment into a small house near Interstate 95, but our real home was South Bend, Indiana. We had only been in Florida for eight months. Both sets of grandparents wanted us to return to Indiana.

"They think I'm helpless," my mother said, "which makes me angry."

We were in the car on a Sunday night, two weeks after my father's funeral, driving home from the beach. My mother was working as a secretary at my brothers' elementary school, and her friends from work had invited us to a cookout. My mother said the cookout was to cheer us up. But, once her friends had got the fire going, they talked about how sad they felt for us. "What kind of food did your father like?" my mother's friend Grace Nolan asked us.

"Meat," Eddie said, "and not many kinds of vegetables."

Grace Nolan started to cry.

"Well, he liked potatoes, too," Lee told her.

"So," my mother said to us now, in the car, "I told your grandparents we'd be staying here."

"Good," Eddie said, from the back seat. Of the three of us—Eddie and Lee and me—he was the one who had made the most friends.

"I'm not sure I want to stay," I told my mother. "Or if Lee does." Lee was asleep, next to Eddie, with his head and shoulders on the seat and the rest of him limp on the floor.

"Lee wants to stay, Jean," my mother said. "I already know that." She pulled up in front of our house. It was ten o'clock, and we had forgotten to leave on any lights.

"Wake up, Lee," my mother said. She got out of the car and opened the back door and gently shook him. Sometimes he slept so soundly that it was impossible to wake him up. He opened his eyes for a moment and looked at the dark house.

"Why isn't Dad home yet?" he asked. My mother picked him up and carried him inside. He and Eddie were small for their ages, whereas I was tall and too heavy. I watched my mother put Lee into bed. Eddie lay down on his own bed, against the opposite wall, and fell asleep with his clothes on.

My mother and I went into the kitchen. Spread out over the table were letters from the construction company my father had worked for, and forms from its insurance company. We were supposed to receive twenty-five thousand dollars, and my mother was planning to use this money to buy the house we were in, which would allow us to live on the salary she made. The problem was that there had been people around, when the accident happened, who said that the fall had been my father's own fault, and not the fault of the construction company. So there was a chance the insurance company might not pay us. My mother was worried about this, and now she sat down at the table and began to fill out the forms.

I went into my room, next to the kitchen, which was really meant to be a small utility room. My father had painted it yellow and put in carpeting for me. I changed into my nightgown and got into bed. Every night since my father died, I had been unable to fall asleep. During the day I didn't cry, and it didn't upset me to hear about things my father had said or done. But as soon as I was almost asleep, memories would come into my mind that made our situation seem real to me. I stayed awake all night, it seemed to me, listening to my mother in the kitchen and to the distant noise of the cars on the highway.

In the morning, my mother made me get up and get ready for school. My brothers and I had stayed home for a week after my father died, and then my mother allowed me to stay home for an additional week. I told her I didn't want to talk to people at school yet, but the truth was also that I had got used to staying home—to being able to wear my nightgown all day if I wanted to, or lie in bed all morning, reading a book. I didn't want to go back to living my life, because my life had started to seem like too much trouble. Each small thing, like brushing my teeth or putting on knee-socks, now made me tired. I felt I had to do fewer things each morning, in order to save energy for some more important thing I might have to do in the afternoon.

After I ate breakfast, I walked to the end of our block and waited for the bus with Nancy Dyer, who was in my class. It was November, and she was wearing a blue corduroy jumper her mother had made. She had brought over my assignments, for the two weeks I had been home, and on the bus we went over them. I made corrections according to the answers she remembered from class. "You did real well," she said when we were finished. "But then, you're smarter than I am to begin with."

"That's not true," I told her. "I just do more homework."

"That's what I mean," she said. She had her eyes on her boyfriend, who was getting on the bus. He was a thin boy, with black hair. He sat in front of us. He ignored her and took out a piece of notebook paper and shot spitballs at a red-haired boy across the aisle.

"He's mad at me all the time now," Nancy whispered. "I don't know why."

She had tears in her eyes, and I looked away and watched the trees flashing past in the window. In the reflection, I could see that three people on the bus were looking at me—the red-haired boy, and two girls in the seat in front of him. When I first got on the bus, one of these girls had said, "There was an announcement in school about your dad."

"I know," I said. "Nancy told me."

"I can't believe that happened to you," she said, and whispered something that I couldn't hear to the other girl. Now, as I turned away from the window and looked across the aisle, the red-haired boy smiled at me and was about to say something when he was hit in the forehead by a spitball.

When we got to school, I went to my locker to put away my sweater, and then I went to science and algebra and history. In each class, the teacher took me aside and talked to me about my father, and two or three other people spoke to me about him as well. The boys, especially, wanted to know exactly what had happened. "Did he step off the beam by accident," one boy asked, "or was there something he tripped over?"

"I think he tripped," I told him.

"Wow," the boy said. "I can just picture that."

During lunch, the group of girls I sat with stopped talking to each other when I walked up. "You can sit here, in the middle," Roberta Price said. Everyone moved over, and Carla Norris unwrapped my straw and put it in my milk. "We wondered when you were coming back," Roberta said. "The principal thought maybe last week."

"I decided to wait until today," I told her. We began to eat. Most of us had bought hot lunches. We all had mothers who were either too busy in the mornings to make us sandwiches or who felt we were old enough now to make them ourselves. Carla was the one exception. Her mother not only made her a sandwich but put a note in with her lunch every day.

"Here it is," Carla said. She unfolded a small piece of yellow paper. "Good luck on your geography quiz," she read out loud. "Your father and I are very proud of you." She and everybody else at the table looked down at their food.

"That's better than the one where she told you to wash off your mascara," I said, after a silence.

"It sure is," Roberta said quickly. "That one was sickening."

I had English class afterward, during fourth period. My English teacher, Mr. Thompson, was sitting at his desk when I walked in. I went to my seat and listened to a boy standing next to Mr. Thompson's desk talk to him about commas. "I don't think we need them," the boy said. "Periods are good enough."

Other people were coming into the room, and Mr. Thompson went up to the blackboard and wrote down a sentence from *A Separate Peace*. The sentence was, "Perhaps I was stopped by that level of feeling, deeper than thought, which contains the truth." After the bell rang, he stepped back from the board and asked, "What, exactly, does this sentence mean?"

Four people he called on said they didn't know. The fifth person said, "I think it means a feeling you keep to yourself."

"Why wouldn't you want anyone to know?" Mr. Thompson asked.

"Because it's a secret," someone else said.

"Maybe it's a secret you keep from yourself," a girl in the back row said. "Maybe people don't want to know their own secrets."

"That doesn't make sense," a boy said.

"A lot of things don't make sense," Mr. Thompson told him, "but they're still true." He gave us an assignment, which we were to do in class, and then he sat on the radiator and watched us work. "Don't forget to use commas," he told us.

After class, I went downstairs to the girls' locker

room to change my clothes for gym. Our teacher was already there, marking off our names as we walked in. She talked to me about my father, and then a girl I knew from another class said, "I don't know what I would do if my father died, even though I hate him."

We all went out to the basketball court and shot baskets from the free-throw line. After gym, I went to the library for study hall, and then I met Nancy in front of my locker, and we walked out to the school bus. Her boyfriend, who got on the bus a few minutes after we did, sat down four rows ahead of us. He spent the whole bus ride talking loudly to a small, blond girl.

"Sometimes people try to hurt you just to see if they can do it," Nancy said.

"You don't know that for sure," I told her.

"Yes, I do," she said. "I've done it to people myself."

We got off at our block and stood for a moment at the corner before we each went home. The air was so still that the traffic from the highway seemed louder than usual. "I guess I don't need to talk to you about feeling sad," Nancy said. "I forgot for a minute."

"It's different with me," I told her. "It's not something you feel every second."

I walked across the neighbors' yard and into our own; I put Lee's bike in the shed and went into the house through the kitchen door. My mother was standing in Lee's doorway, and I heard Lee say, "I got an A in spelling. Dad gave me fifty cents last time."

My mother gave Lee two quarters, and then she walked past me into the kitchen, opened the kitchen door, and sat outside on our steps. I went out and sat beside her. "Did Dad really give Lee fifty cents?" she asked me.

"I thought it was a quarter," I told her, "but I might be remembering it wrong." She held my hand, and we watched a squirrel race around the shed.

"Would you give me a hug, honey?" she asked. I put my arms around her. In the past year, I had grown a lot, and now I was bigger than she was; when I hugged her, I was able to put my arms all the way around her.

"I wish I'd stop growing," I told her.

"You'll be tall, like Dad was," she said. "Someday you'll appreciate it." She stood up and walked down into the yard. She was still dressed in her work clothes— a skirt and blouse and high heels—and her shoes were invisible in the long grass. No one had mowed the yard since my father had died. "The lawn will have to be Eddie's job now," my mother said. "You and Lee can do the raking." She looked up toward the clatter of a woodpecker in our sweet-gum tree. "I'll find a gas station that will change the oil in the car, and then I'll teach myself to do the other things Dad did."

"That seems like a lot," I told her.

"I know it does, honey." She sat back down beside me and pulled up weeds that were growing out of the cracks in the steps. I looked around at the yard and the house—at the patches of bare ground under the trees, the peeling paint around the windows, and all the small holes in the screens—and thought that it would take an army of men to fix everything that was broken.

My mother and I went inside to peel potatoes. At six o'clock, when Eddie came home from playing football with his friends, we all had supper in the kitchen.

"I made a touchdown today," Eddie said.

"Well, good for you," my mother said. "I wish I could have seen it." She had eaten quickly, and she put her plate in the sink and drank a cup of instant coffee while she watched us finish.

Afterward, I cleared the table and washed the dishes. I forgot that it was Eddie's turn, and he didn't remind me until I was done. He and Lee were sitting on the floor in the living room, with Lee's toy soldiers all around them. They were watching television with my mother. I came into the room and said, "I don't feel like watching TV."

"Who cares?" Eddie asked.

"We all care," my mother said sharply. "We're a family, even without Dad. We care what happens to each other." The way she spoke and the look on her face reminded me of my father, of the times he'd lost his temper with us. Eddie and Lee looked surprised, and then, a second later, there were tears on their faces.

I was crying, too, because my mother had started to cry. But I wasn't upset about what Eddie had said or because my mother had got angry. I startled myself by feeling almost glad. It seemed to me that all of a sudden our lives were ordinary again, except that my father wasn't there, and I felt like I was paying attention after being lost in a daydream, or like I was opening my eyes after seeing how long I could keep them closed. When my mother started to speak, I hoped she wouldn't say something nice that would cancel out her angry words. But what she said was, "Okay. Pick up these toys. Then we're going to turn off the television and go to bed."

It was only seven-thirty, but we went into our rooms. I didn't bother to put on my nightgown. I took off my clothes and got into bed in my underwear, and, even though it was early, I didn't have my same trouble falling asleep. I knew now that my father was dead and that we would live our lives without him, and I fell asleep right away, so that for a while I could not know these things.

Moving

A year and a half after my father died, my mother began dating Mr. Thompson, a teacher from my junior high school. It was 1968, and I had just turned fifteen. My mother and my brothers and I were living in Jacksonville, Florida, but before and after my mother dated Mr. Thompson, when she was feeling especially lonely, she talked about moving to the West, to South Dakota or Wyoming. Those sounded like lonely places to me. That was why she thought of them, I decided; it seemed to me that the answer to loneliness, for my mother, was to find more of it.

She met Mr. Thompson at a Christmas party for Jacksonville public school employees—she worked as a secretary at Lee's elementary school—and what she and Mr. Thompson had in common was me. The morning after the party, she told me that he had said I was intelligent, and nice.

"That was all he said?" I asked her.

"What more do you want, Jean?" my mother said. "Those are wonderful compliments."

We were in the kitchen, and she was making pancakes for my brothers and me. She let me turn the radio to a rock and roll station, and she was more patient than usual with Lee, who was zooming little metal airplanes down low over the table. But as the day went on she seemed less happy, and talked less about the party. It was months before Mr. Thompson called her; when he did call it was a surprise to her because she hadn't seen him again.

It was May, and already hot. Our small house didn't have air conditioning except in my mother's bedroom, where we all slept on the hottest nights. The yard was overgrown with wild rose bushes and bougainvillea. My mother and Eddie would go out with rakes and pruning shears and come in scratched and bloody, and then two weeks later the plants would take over again. We were used to our old home—South Bend, Indiana—where things grew at normal rates and died off completely in the winter. Here we felt that we'd entered a horror movie such as *Them*. One night I would be sitting next to an open window, watching television, and the next night, sitting in the same chair, a vine that hadn't been there before would be tickling my neck.

My mother's first date with Mr. Thompson was on a rainy night. He came inside and my mother introduced him to my brothers. She was wearing a pink dress and white high heels, and I could see the embarrassment on her face as he helped her on with her raincoat—a gray slicker she'd had as long as I could remember, that she used to wear on our camping trips. Mr. Thompson seemed shy around me. He asked me about ninth grade and if I were excited about high school.

After he and my mother left, Eddie told me he didn't like Mr. Thompson, though he didn't give a reason why, and Lee was confused about why she was with him. "Did you do something wrong when he was your teacher?" Lee asked me.

"Of course not," I said. "Mom's not with him to talk about me. She's just going to a movie with him, for fun."

We had ice cream, and then we watched television until it was time for my brothers to go to bed. I was reading when my mother got home. She came into my room and said, "Why didn't you talk more about Mr. Thompson when you were in his class? He's one of the most interesting people I've ever met."

"I just thought of him as a teacher," I told her.

My mother closed my curtains. "There's so much more to him than that," she said. "You learn a lot about someone when you're on a date, Jean. You'll find that out when you start having dates yourself."

My friends were already having dates, which my mother hadn't noticed. At school that year we were having a unit on genetics in biology class; the fact that my mother was dating and I wasn't made me think there was a popularity gene and I hadn't inherited it.

"What did you talk about with Mr. Thompson?" I asked her. "Did you talk about Dad?"

"Oh, no," she said. "Well, not exactly. Mr. Thompson just said that he knew we must miss him. Then we talked about our jobs, and about hobbies. Mr. Thompson likes deep-sea fishing."

"I know," I told her. "He used to talk about that."

"You see?" my mother said. "You did learn something about him."

After she left my room, I put down my book and turned out the light. On certain nights I knew in advance that I would dream about my father—if something bad happened at school, or if my mother and brothers and I were talking about him a lot. Or if, like now, I felt that things were happening that wouldn't be if my father were still alive. That night I dreamed my father was sitting in our living room, looking out the window at the darkness. It was exactly what he used to do, and so it took me a few minutes after I woke up to realize that it had been a dream and not reality.

Mr. Thompson began going out with my mother every weekend, and he was sometimes at our house during the week—to have dinner with us or to help my mother repair something. Before dinner one evening, while my mother was cooking, Mr. Thompson came onto the front porch, where I was reading. "I don't think I've ever seen you without a book," he said. "What are you reading now?"

"*Winesburg, Ohio,*" I told him.

"Do you like it?" he asked me.

"I like it a lot," I said. "It reminds me of Indiana."

Mr. Thompson sat down on the top step. "You must get homesick," he said. "It's hard to move at your age."

"Well, I miss my grandparents," I told him. "I miss having more people around our house."

"It makes things less lonely, doesn't it?" he said. "It cheers everybody up."

My mother called us in for dinner, and after we ate, Mr. Thompson played football with my brothers. "See how good he is with children?" my mother said, as she and I were putting away the leftovers. Mr. Thompson and my brothers were in the back yard, and we could see them through the screen door.

"But they're not his own children," I told her. "It's probably easier to pay attention to children if they don't belong to you."

"Honey, are you thinking about Dad?" my mother asked me.

"Maybe," I said. "Sort of, I guess."

"Dad just had things on his mind that he needed to think about," my mother said.

"Like what?" I asked her.

"Well, he didn't feel he was a success," my mother said. "He never found anything he was good at." My father had had a lot of different kinds of jobs; he had never worked at the same place for more than three years. My mother handed me the sponge so that I could wipe off the table. "Honey, Dad was disappointed in himself," she told me.

We finished cleaning up the kitchen and went outside. The sun had gone down an hour before, but Mr. Thompson and my brothers were still playing. Mr. Thompson never missed when my brothers threw the football to him, and he threw it back perfectly each time. The three of them moved closer together in order to see each other in the growing darkness.

My best friend that year was Nancy Dyer, who lived two blocks away. She was my age, but she had had boyfriends since the sixth grade. She was now going out with a seventeen-year-old boy who had quit school and was living in a house with some other boys. She said that he was thinking about going to California, and that he would take her with him. "He said we would live on a beach somewhere," Nancy told me.

"What about school, and your parents?" I asked her.

"Well, I don't care about school, and I don't get along with my mother the way that you do," she said. "I would miss my dad. But I have to think about my future."

On a Monday night when I told my mother I was going to the library, I went with Nancy to her boyfriend's house. There was another boy there, also seventeen, who I talked to while Nancy and her boyfriend were in the bedroom. The boy I talked to didn't seem interested in me except when I told him about how my father had died—falling from a building at a construction site. "I bet that was something, how he felt on the way down," he said. "People use drugs to feel like that."

"Do you?" I asked him.

"Only marijuana and LSD, so far," he said. We were sitting on a couch in the living room, and he put his arm around me for just a moment. It was the first time I'd ever had a boy do that, and later, as Nancy and I were walking home, I thought about how my father used to sometimes sit like that with me, and I wondered how he would feel if he knew I was with boys now—whether he would be happy for me, or whether he would be disappointed in me in the way that he'd been disappointed in himself.

"Don't you think those guys are cool?" Nancy said.

"It makes me feel older to be with them, because they're so mature."

We were half a block from my house. Mr. Thompson's car was parked in front, and I could see him and my mother sitting together on the front steps. My brothers were probably in bed, and the house was dark except for a lamp in the living room, shining through the white curtain and spilling a little light on my mother, who was kissing Mr. Thompson. I stopped walking, and I took Nancy's arm and turned her around, and we went back to the corner and walked around the block; I was hoping that by the time we got to the house, my mother and Mr. Thompson would have pulled apart from each other.

Once school was out for the summer, I had to stay home and take care of my brothers. Eddie went out with his friends and only came home sometimes for lunch, but Lee played either in his room or in the yard. I sat outside and read, or, if Lee was in a good mood, helped him with his reading. He didn't do well in school; he didn't like it, and he got angry when he didn't understand something. He had a bad temper, and when he got mad at me I was tempted to say, "You're just like Dad," except that I felt guilty having that thought about my father.

Mr. Thompson was the only person who could help Lee without Lee getting mad. They would sit together at the kitchen table after dinner, with a book like *Charlotte's Web,* and Lee would slowly make his way through a page while Mr. Thompson listened, making corrections. My mother and Eddie and I stayed out of the room, since Lee said we made him nervous. Eddie watched television while my mother and I sat outside. Often, I was waiting for Nancy to come by and get me; we lied to my mother about where we were going so that we could visit Nancy's boyfriend again.

"Look at the June bugs," my mother said on one of these evenings. It was dusk, and the grass and trees were full of the sounds of crickets and cicadas.

"I'd hate to step on one," I told her. "They're so big it would be like stepping on a little animal."

"They're interesting, though," my mother said. "Some people study insects. I think that's a subject I might have chosen if I had gone to college."

"Why didn't you go to college?" I asked her.

"My family and Dad's family didn't think about things like college," she told me. "It was too expensive. And Dad and I didn't get the good grades you do." She nudged one of the June bugs with the toe of her shoe. "Dad and I were a little bit wild when we were in high school," my mother said. "I'm glad you're not. I don't like to remember how much I made my own mother worry."

We saw Nancy walking down the sidewalk toward us, carrying a book, and my mother smiled at her and waved. "Don't you look pretty," she said, when Nancy got closer. Nancy was wearing a blue sundress.

"Thank you," Nancy said. "It's brand new. And I'm not wearing anything under it," she whispered to me a few minutes later, after we had walked away from my mother.

At Nancy's boyfriend's house, the boy I had talked to before was there again. I had seen him one other time, since the night he had put his arm around me, and he hadn't paid attention to me. I thought it was because he was out of my league; if he did notice me, I thought, it would mean I had changed—had gotten prettier or more likeable. He sat down next to me after Nancy and her boyfriend left the room. The radio was on, and he said, "I like this," meaning the song that was playing.

"I do, too," I told him. "What other songs do you like?"

"You mean groups?" he said. "Don't you know who's playing, when you hear a song?"

"I mean groups," I told him. "I don't know why I said 'songs.'"

"The Rolling Stones." He looked away from me with a bored expression. He had thin, wavy hair that fell over his eyes. He tapped his fingers on the arm of the couch, and then he slowly lifted his hand and put it on my knee. He started tapping his fingers on the cuff of my shorts. "Most of the groups are not that good," he said. "Only one or two of them can really play."

"Really?" I said. "How do you know that?"

"Everybody knows that," he said. He stopped tapping his fingers, and he moved his hand up slightly on my leg. He had given me a beer, earlier, and I held it on the leg he wasn't touching and forgot to drink it. Later, when Nancy and her boyfriend came back into the room, he took away his hand to reach for the beer Nancy's boyfriend was handing him.

Nancy sat down next to me. Her hair was tangled and the sash on her dress was untied, and she seemed unhappy, the way she often did after she spent time alone with a boy. "It's ten o'clock," she said to me. "Every night at ten, my father says to my mother, 'Do you know where your children are?'"

"Why?" her boyfriend asked her.

"As a joke," she said. "My father likes to make us laugh."

"Then he should say something funny," her boyfriend said.

"I don't notice you saying anything so funny," Nancy told him, "or trying so hard to make me laugh."

"Hey," her boyfriend said, in a hurt voice. Nancy stood up and crossed the room and sat on his lap, but she was looking out the window, and I felt that in her mind she was already with the next boyfriend, and that she and I wouldn't be coming here anymore.

"It was nice to meet you," I said to the boy I was with.

"What?" he said. He and Nancy's boyfriend looked at me as though I'd turned into someone else—an adult they didn't like, such as a policeman or a parent.

Mr. Thompson's car wasn't in front of our house when I got home. He didn't come over the next night, or the night after that. My mother said he was making repairs on his house, but Saturday at breakfast, after my brothers had gone outside, she said, "Mr. Thompson and I had an argument. I don't think we're going to see each other anymore."

"Why not?" I asked her. "Why can't you just make up?"

"Because we hurt each other's feelings, Jean," she said, "like Dad and I used to." She pushed away her plate, and I helped her clear the table and put away the cereal boxes. Then she went into her bedroom and closed the door.

I went outside and watched my brothers try to build a fort in the backyard. They were arguing about how to do it. "Mr. Thompson can help us next time he comes over," Lee said.

"He probably won't come here again," Eddie said. "I don't think he and Mom still like each other."

"Why not?" Lee asked.

"How should I know?" Eddie picked up my father's hammer and started nailing two boards together, and Lee came over and sat down next to me. I had brought a book outside, which I didn't feel like reading, and he opened it to the first page and then closed it and carefully put it on the top step beside him.

After a while, my mother came outside. "I'm going to run some errands," she told us.

"Can I come?" Lee asked.

"Not today," she told him. "I'm not in a good mood, Lee. I wouldn't be good company."

She came home later with groceries and dry cleaning, and as she put things away she began talking again about moving to Wyoming or South Dakota. She said she didn't like how hot and rainy it was in Florida, and she had decided it wasn't a good place for us to grow up. "I don't think we fit in here," she said. She had gone to the library and brought home copies of the *National Geographic* that had articles about the West, and she sat us down in the living room that evening, after dinner, and showed them to us. My brothers got excited about the pictures of ranchers on horseback. I liked the photographs of the sky at sunrise and sunset, but I didn't like all the emptiness beneath the sky, and I thought the mountains, though they were pretty, would be frightening up close.

"See how much we would be on our own out there?" my mother said. "If we didn't do well, it would be our own fault. We would have no one to blame but ourselves."

"What would be so good about that?" I asked her.

"We would be independent," she said. "We wouldn't have to rely on anyone else." She gave my brothers another magazine to look at, and she went outside to smoke a cigarette. Smoking was something she hadn't done when my father was alive; it was one more thing, I felt, that put our life with him farther behind us, as though he were a town we left and could never go back to. I followed her outside and she said, "That was one of Dad's problems. He was afraid to trust himself."

It was dark outside; it was after nine o'clock and the street was empty, and instead of thinking about the way my father had died, as I often did when people mentioned him, I thought about how unsure he must have felt standing on top of the building. I imagined him thinking, I'll probably make a mistake now, the way I've made mistakes before.

My mother was telling me about a school in South Dakota that needed a secretary, but I didn't want to hear about it. I was listening to the cicadas and crickets and thinking about how, when I was older, I would come back to Florida. I would just stay here in one place my whole life.

Prisoners
of Love

Mourning Doves

My mother, Lorraine, fell in love with Wayne Lissell at the Paradise Valley K-Mart. She was trying on sneakers while I spied on my stepbrother, Lewis. He was scouting the lingerie department, watching women choose underwear and closing in on a blonde checking out a pair of red panties. He pretended to be fascinated by some striped pajamas with feet. Lewis had on a madras shirt that had belonged to his father in the sixties, and I happened to know that when it wasn't tucked in it covered his knees. Lewis was five feet tall, and fine-boned. He flirted with girls in a relentless way, like this blonde he was moving closer to, ready to deliver the big punch line. I called his name as if I were calling in a dog for dinner, and he jumped and backed off. By the time we reached Lorraine, she was on the floor between six pairs of sneakers and Wayne Lissell, this cowboy/hardware man from Tulsa. He was chewing gum and smiling as Lorraine introduced us. Lorraine's own shoes—brown open-toed, high-heeled sandals—lay suggestively on the floor near his feet.

On the way home, Lewis drove. I sat in the back and listened to a discussion about Lewis's room, which he was papering with black felt. "You think it's going to drive the girls crazy," Lorraine said. "You think they're going to see those fuzzy walls and jump out of their pants, Lewis. You're nineteen and you're crazy. That's okay, that's how it is when you're nineteen. But take it from your mother—girls are going to see those walls and run like hell. Ask your sister, Lewis."

He didn't ask me. He lit a cigarette and closed his window. Lorraine and I opened windows. He started combing his hair in the rearview mirror into his peculiar punk rooster style.

"Drop me off at my apartment and come back when you're thirty," I told him.

"Bleu!" Lorraine said. She named me Bleu, after the cheese.

"I have to go to work," I said. "I told Mr. Hall I'd fill in tonight for a girl who got pregnant." Mr. Hall managed the Phoenix resort where I worked as a waitress. He was also Billy's father. Billy was the man I used to date; he was dead.

"That man would do anything for you," Lorraine said. "He told me that."

I didn't say anything; Mr. Hall was none of her business. I was missing a biology class, which made me feel bad. I took college classes on my nights off; Billy had talked me into it, then I started to like it. "Come back when you're forty-nine," I told Lewis.

A few days later, Mr. Hall and I were having dinner out, and Lorraine and Wayne Lissell were in the bar. Wayne was a big man—six-three maybe, blond, with a moustache, and a gold coin for a belt buckle. He had large blue eyes that moved around a lot.

"This is Lewis's first night with the walls and a girl—what's-her-name," Lorraine told us. "He's got the left-over felt stuffed in the garbage. Wayne says Lewis is a character."

Wayne had his arm around her like he was used to being quoted. He snapped his fingers for a waitress, and Mr. Hall and I sort of shuddered.

"Honey, call her over," Lorraine told him. "You're giving Bleu and Mr. Hall here high blood pressure."

"Sweetheart!" Wayne called out to the waitress. "Sugar!"

"I wish Lewis would turn twenty-five real quick," Lorraine said.

"I worried about Billy all the time, and it didn't prevent a thing," Mr. Hall said. "It didn't make a bit of difference. My son was killed in an automobile accident," he told Wayne. "A sports car. I tried to talk him out of that little car. I offered to buy him something more substantial. The only thing I found out was that when you love someone you better protect yourself. I mean emotionally." Mr. Hall was small, delicate-looking, and handsome.

"Mr. Hall, you get hurt anyway," Lorraine said.

"Yes, you do. I know that. You can't protect yourself from all the things you did wrong in the past. I think that's the pain, right there." Wayne lit a cigarette.

49

"That's what gets you," Mr. Hall said. He spread his hands on the table. He had very nice hands, with long fingers. He spread them apart as far as possible.

"I miss your Billy," Lorraine said. "To this day, sometimes I'll be at Bleu's and find myself thinking Billy must be asleep in the bedroom."

"I'm a fortunate man. I've never lost anybody," Wayne told us.

"I'll tell you what I've been meaning to say to Bleu," Lorraine said. "It seems to me that if you miss someone so much you keep thinking he's still there, then he is still there."

"You forget he's dead," Wayne said.

"Wayne, you don't forget someone you love is dead, honey. What I'm saying is, it's like if you were standing in an empty room you'd say it felt empty, but what you'd feel is more of yourself or the chairs or something. It's like that." Lorraine helped herself to Wayne's cigarettes. "Hey, I'm not talking about ghosts."

Mr. Hall was opening and closing his hands as if they hurt, watching himself do it.

"She's always talking about love," Wayne said.

"What happens is you talk about it when you don't know you're talking about it," Lorraine said.

"That's right," Mr. Hall said.

"You've got a great boss, baby," Lorraine told me. "And he had a wonderful son." She leaned over and kissed Mr. Hall on the cheek.

"I'll tell you what," Wayne said. "I need another drink. Do me a favor, sweetheart," he told Lorraine. "Hold back on some of that love."

. . .

A week later, Lewis told me Lorraine was acting funny. "She doesn't eat, she doesn't sleep. At four in the morning she's cleaning the oven. She's turned into some crazy broad." I was at work and he was sitting in my section having a Coke. He was wearing a maroon silk shirt he bought at the Salvation Army for a dollar. His hair was wet.

Mr. Hall came over to say hello. He shook hands with Lewis. "My mother's wacko," Lewis said.

"She's in love with Wayne," I told him.

Lewis raised his eyebrows—never an effective gesture for him, because they were so pale. I tried to tell him that once; he was offended. "Wonderful," Lewis said. He rolled up his napkin and acted like he was going to toss it at an elderly couple across the room. Mr. Hall took it away from him.

"Look at my teeth," Lewis said. "I spent twenty bucks on this stuff I sent away for to make them white, and I think they're turning green. When I was in L.A. with my dad, the whole city was filled with teeth so white it hurt your head. I looked for a job. Those applications had two blanks—one for your name, and one for the color of your teeth. Someday I'll get them capped or paint them or something and get a job in show business."

After he left, Mr. Hall picked up the remains of Lewis's placemat. "I wouldn't mind believing in white teeth," he said. "It would be so easy." I went to check on the old couple.

Wayne Lissell's sixteen-year-old son, Ray, rode in on

the bus for a surprise visit, and Wayne brought him over to Lorraine's for dinner. He was almost as big as Wayne, and had a long, doglike face. Lewis and I watched him swallow two Quaaludes in the bathroom before we ate. He was wearing his high-school letter jacket. After he took the pills, he wet his hair down and combed it carefully, making a little wave in the front.

We had pot roast. Ray had three helpings, and then excused himself and went outside and fell down on the grass. "He's so relaxed," Lorraine said. "He makes himself right at home. Wouldn't you like to be like that, Lewis? Lewis is always running around in first gear," she told Wayne.

Outside, Ray was on his back piling grass on his chest. After a while, he started rolling all over like a big pipe. In the kitchen, Lorraine and I were doing dishes; Lorraine had on a red apron and very red lipstick. She motioned me over to the window. The patio light was on; the evening sky was a bright dark blue—the color of outer space. We watched Ray roll all the way from the left side of the yard to the right and back again, in a slightly diagonal pattern. "Look at what he's doing," Lorraine whispered. "Jesus, I hope this isn't some kind of weird revelation from God about my life."

In the end, Wayne Lissell returned to his wife/ex-wife. "He packed up his nuts and bolts and took his ass back to Tulsa," Lewis told me in an emergency phone call. I drove over, and Lewis and I performed a little sunset ceremony. We lit the charcoal grill and burned a shirt Wayne had left behind, along with the state of Oklahoma, which Lewis cut out of the atlas. Lorraine stood outside in her mourning-for-men outfit, an old tent dress with poodles on it. In back of us, the sun sat on the horizon like an Italian tomato.

"You'll have to set me on fire, too," Lorraine said.

Lewis rocked back on his heels and poked at the remains of Wayne's shirt with a stick. He was nervous. His former girlfriend, Darlene, had lost control one night at a 7-Eleven and tried to hold up the cashier with an emery board. She was institutionalized somewhere. Lorraine patted him on the head and went inside to calm herself with some vodka.

After dinner, Lewis and I insisted that she change clothes and go out with us to the Blue Owl. Lewis had an I.D., which he flashed impatiently, lighting a cigarette while they looked at it. He was wearing a tight shirt unbuttoned halfway, and tight red pants. Lorraine had changed into a green jumpsuit and cowboy boots. She looked tired but okay. Two or three men at the bar were eyeing her. A country-and-western band was tuning up; the lead singer had the kind of body Lewis would have sacrificed white teeth for. We sat in front and ordered pitchers.

"He had a big heart," Lorraine said. This was after her fourth trip to the ladies' room and a few philosophical exchanges with the barstool men on the way.

Lewis, not the drinker he liked to think he was, was swallowing directly out of the pitcher. "His heart was so big he deserved a harem," Lewis said. "He should have been king somewhere, he was such a hell of a guy. He was so great I was falling in love with him—I was going to propose the night he left."

"He had some wonderful qualities," Lorraine said. Her eyes were wet.

"He was a jerk!" Lewis shouted.

Lorraine grabbed his arm. "Don't tell your mother about men," she said. "His wife was holding something over his head. He couldn't tell me what it was. Something big."

One of the barstool men came over and asked Lorraine to dance. "I'd rather die first," she said. She smoothed her hair and put on lipstick, missing part of her bottom lip. She wiped it off and tried again. Lewis was shouting something at the band in Spanish. "Lewis is speaking a foreign language," Lorraine said. "What the hell are you saying, Lewis?"

"The song sucks," Lewis said.

"Such a lovely song," Lorraine told him. "I turn up the radio when this song comes on."

Lewis was getting wound up. He was on his feet, climbing on top of the table. "Here's the song I want you to play," he told the band. "It's from the movie *Hawaii*. You dumb-asses never heard of it." He had his hands in his hair, scrubbing, and his hips were going like a washing machine. Everyone was clapping and yelling except the band, who had seen too many Lewises. They took a break and filed past us without even looking up.

After Lewis was thrown out, Lorraine drove him home. I stayed and had a few drinks with the lead singer. His name was Buddy, and he drove me back to my place. Buddy liked good wine. He had lived in Australia for six months, and he had a small tattoo on his left shoulder, which he regretted.

"Tell me what makes you feel good," he said. We were undressed, lying on my living-room rug. The TV was on without the sound; the room was blue in the light. I was pretty drunk.

"I don't know," I said. "Maybe doing those experiments in biology lab with the bacteria swimming around under the microscope. Things you can figure out."

Buddy sat up. "Biology lab?" he said, shaking his head. "I've never heard that one." He put his hand on my back. "What makes me feel good is to touch a girl like this and not have to think about anything else," he said.

I started to cry, thinking about Billy. "Well," Buddy said. He started to scratch my back in careful circles, as if he were tracing half-dollars or drawing with a compass. "If you need to fall in love with somebody, make it me," he said. "I never hurt anybody. I'm not a perfect person or anything, I'm just not dangerous."

Lorraine was upset about Wayne for a long time. I'd seen her survive a lot of men, better men, but this was different. "Because I'm older," she said. "I mean business now. I'm not some deer for men to shoot at." We were at my apartment, finishing lunch.

"You look good," I told her. She had her hair done a new way.

"I look okay," she said. "I've tried to pull myself together for Lewis's sake. I can see he's still thinking about that crazy Darlene. Watch out for love, baby." She got up and helped herself to a beer.

What I knew about love was how it felt bouncing off someone who'd disappeared. I leaned back and put my feet up on the coffee table. "You've been in love at least a dozen times that I know of," I told Lorraine. "Of course, I'm counting a lot of quick infatuations in there, like the time you went crazy over the guy who yanked out the mailbox."

"Harry," Lorraine said. "He did that because he loved me so much." She offered me a sip of her beer.

"And the one with the skin disease?"

Lorraine gave me her beer and got another one for herself. "Count him twice," she said. "He was really something. And I'll tell you, honey—he loved me. He loved me, and what's more he didn't want to kill me." She stood up and smoothed down her slacks. "I'm getting chunky," she said. "I was watching Lewis this morning. Honey, he shouldn't wear stripes. He looks so skinny, like some of that striped toothpaste." She put her beer down and picked up her purse. "Well, I've got to go and meet somebody."

He was Charles Crouch, the owner of a car dealership and a gourmet cook. He had us all over for dinner one night and served mourning doves on little nests of spinach and rice. Lorraine and I got three apiece; Lewis, Charles, and Mr. Hall each got four. They were steaming hot. It was like they'd been asleep in their nests and then were suddenly zapped in the microwave.

Lewis was looking at his plate open-mouthed. His teeth looked great. He was in the process of having them bleached—a new dental procedure. He'd just had a permanent, and his hair curled close to his head. It was a lighter blond—almost white. "We can't eat these," he said. "These are birds, man. This is what you eat when you're lost in the jungle and you finished off your leather boots the day before."

"I'm sure they're delicious," Mr. Hall said.

"Look at their little wings." Lorraine picked one up with her napkin and held it up to the light. "You never get to see birds real close like this."

Charles started to eat one of his while we all watched. He put it down. We were staring at the buckshot hole in its side. "I've got some pasta and some cheddar cheese, and they were both dead when I bought them," he said. "I'm going to throw something together."

While Charles was in the kitchen, Lewis buried all the birds in the yard. From the patio, he took a small cactus in a pot and used it for a headstone.

Mr. Hall got up and wandered around Charles's living room, a big place with leather furniture and glass tables. He sat in a red chair with his legs crossed and started to read a *Gourmet* magazine. He cleared his throat a few times. He had had a chronic sinus problem since Billy died, and now it was part of his personality, like a gesture. "Bleu," he said, "let's show this recipe to Marcel." Marcel was the chef at the restaurant. Mr. Hall held up the magazine and showed me a picture of a lamb stew. I nodded. Every once in a while I sort of fell in love with him, which made me feel like we were fused together in some extraordinary way, like jets refueling in midair.

Lewis had walked out of the yard into the desert. Charles's house was on the edge of a new subdivision. It was very dark out—no moon, no stars. "I think I can see Lewis's teeth out there picking up light from a spacecraft or something," I told Mr. Hall.

"He'll be pleased to hear that," Mr. Hall said. "Here's a good recipe for ratatouille. You'd like it, Bleu. I'm going to make it for you sometime." I sat on the floor and looked at my reflection in the window. "Filet of sole with lobster tail," Mr. Hall said. "How does that sound to you?"

"Good," I said. Through my reflection I could see Lewis coming back, stepping carefully over the birds' graves, wiping his hands on his jeans.

"What do you think of cats who eat birds?" Lewis asked Mr. Hall when he came in.

"Cats?" Mr. Hall said. "Mr. Crouch has cats?"

Lewis put one foot up on the edge of the coffee table, tightened his belt, and lit a cigarette. "A guy. A man," Lewis said. "You know, a cat—*Crouch.*"

"Oh, yes," Mr. Hall said. "I can't keep up with you, Lewis." He motioned for him to take his foot off the table. "Well," he said, "I think Lorraine's safe with him—she's too big to cook. He seems all right to me, Lewis. People who cook well tend to be careful about what they do."

"Those little wings," Lewis said. "Like a baby's fingernails or something. Nightmare material. I'm going to dream about those suckers for years. That's how I am. When something freaks me out, it digs a little spinach-and-rice nest here by my heart." Lewis outlined a circle on his chest. Mr. Hall moved an ashtray under Lewis's cigarette a second before the ash would have fallen on a translucent green vase.

"I'm really in love this time," Lorraine told me. We were at the Blue Owl with Lewis, who had been reinstated with Buddy's influence, and Mr. Hall. "Charles'll be here later, honey, and I want you to notice his shoes. I've never known a man with such beautiful shoes. That means something." Lewis rolled his eyes, and Lorraine patted him on the knee. "Have faith in your mother, baby," she told him. "And forget about those little birds." She called the waitress over and ordered herself a Southern Comfort Manhattan with an extra cherry.

We were sitting right up in front at a small table covered with the band's drinks. Lorraine had on three silver bracelets. "Honey, I feel great," she said. "I feel like I'm in the movies. Take a look at my teeth, Lewis. Are they movie material?" She winked at Mr. Hall.

Lewis shielded his eyes with his hand. "Man, you're blinding me," he said. "I must be in Hollywood with the stars." Lewis was wearing a white Western shirt with a red bandanna around his neck. "I'm in a front-row seat at the Academy Awards."

"We need to find you a girl, Lewis," Lorraine said.

Lewis tilted back his chair. "I can live without broads," he told us. "I can go to Tibet and live up in the mountains in a cave. I can be a rock star and use drugs. Anyway, she'd have to be rich."

Lorraine put out one of Lewis's cigarettes. He had two going. "I mentioned your name to the little redhead at the meat market," she told him.

"Okay," he said.

Mr. Hall and I were drinking stingers and holding hands, which was just a thing we did sometimes. After a while, he put both his arms around me and sang the songs along with Buddy. Mr. Hall liked country-and-western—all those people who break your heart and leave you with a little healthy sadness, or a lot, even. They were good songs, and if you were drunk enough they'd make you cry. And then you'd feel better.

In One Place

The Real-West Mobile Home Park, Wynn's home for twenty-five years, is on the edge of town near the state line, sandwiched between a cemetery and the highway. On the other side of the highway is the J & S Tavern, where Wynn and Annalee work. Wynn, who's fifty-four, lives in the trailer next to Annalee's. The two of them are outside, working on a small vegetable garden. Wynn has his television turned up so that he and Annalee can listen to a quiz program.

"True or false," the master of ceremonies says. "The title of Neil Sedaka's 1962 hit song, 'Breaking Up Is Hard to Do,' was originally written by Shakespeare." There's the sound of a buzzer. "True!" a man shouts. "No, I'm very sorry," says the MC, "that is *not* true. Your opponent receives fifty points."

"I don't know anything about Shakespeare," Wynn says, "but I sure as hell know he didn't say that." He's wearing jeans and work boots and a new blue plaid shirt.

Annalee is sorting through a box of seed packets. She has a swollen lip; her boyfriend punched her this morning because she had run out of bacon. She walks over to Wynn's truck and inspects her lip in the side-view mirror. "It's really strange to have somebody hit you," she says. "When I was in high school, a boy hit me once and I remember thinking, If he hits me again I'm going to kill him. Then he hit me again and I didn't do anything."

"That's because you never learned to watch out for yourself," Wynn says. He lights a cigarette and studies the paint job on his truck, which has turned out greener than he intended. "You could start right now."

"I can't help loving him," Annalee says. "It's just how I feel."

"Well, if he hits you again, he'll have me to answer to. I want you to tell him that."

"Okay," Annalee says. She's unwrapping a candy bar that was in the pocket of her jeans and is against the rules of her diet. In the past year, she's lost thirty pounds, and Wynn figures she has thirty more to lose before she'll get a fair shake from life. Annalee is twenty-four.

They work in the garden for another hour, until the wind picks up and the woman across the street calls for her children. Annalee is shivering. They collect their garden tools in a cardboard box and store it underneath Annalee's trailer. Then they get ready for school. Annalee and Wynn are taking classes in order to earn their high-school diplomas.

· · ·

A little after seven, they climb into Wynn's truck and drive into Dixon. The sun has set behind Moon Hill, which isn't one hill but a ridge of hills that are gray-blue in the evening, as if there might be rain or smoke in the distance. Annalee has her science book open on her lap, and in the remaining light is studying for a test. "What would happen if you were sitting in a room and it suddenly filled with methane?" she asks Wynn.

"You'd explode," Wynn says.

"No, you wouldn't. You'd just die. For a few seconds you'd feel as though you were falling asleep, and then you'd just be unconscious." She closes her book. "You wouldn't feel anything. You wouldn't even have time to think about what you'd miss."

Wynn pulls into the school parking lot and they wait in the truck until class time; most of the students are in their teens and make Wynn and Annalee feel out of place. In the car next to them, four boys wearing bandannas on their heads are passing around a whiskey bottle. They have the doors open and they're talking about girls.

"Number one, their language is disgusting," Wynn says, "and number two, they don't know what they're talking about." He's proofreading a tongue-in-cheek composition he wrote entitled "The Importance of Vowels," which took him four hours to write. "I can't believe it," he tells Annalee. "This isn't funny. I can't understand what happened—it was funny as hell while I was writing it." He puts a comma after the title and adds the words "A Humorous Essay."

After their classes, Wynn and Annalee stop at a drive-in for hamburgers and then visit Wynn's parents, who live south of Dixon in a green frame house they've been in for fifty-two years. They're watching a television movie about call girls in New York City. Wynn and Annalee sit on the couch and watch the rest of the movie with them.

"The little blond girl is being followed by a man who killed another girl earlier on," Wynn's father explains. "Look at her—she's going to open the door for a complete stranger."

"In her nightgown," Wynn's mother adds.

During a commercial, Wynn's father turns down the volume with the remote control and Wynn's mother serves coffee. His parents drink coffee day and night, and each has a special cup. Wynn's father's cup came as a bonus with a box of breakfast cereal. Wynn helps his mother sit down, which is becoming difficult for her. Before long, Wynn thinks, he'll have to build a ramp from the walkway to the front porch.

"Next time I come over, I'll fix the railing. Meanwhile," Wynn says, motioning to the porch, "don't lean on it. It'll give way and you'll end up in the bushes."

"Don't worry about us," Wynn's father says.

"Then listen to what I'm saying. Did you hear what I said?"

"You told us not to fall off the porch." His father turns up the volume for the movie. He's ninety-one. He's wearing high-top basketball sneakers that help support his ankles, and a blue cap. He has a collection of threadbare caps in the utility room, which hang from the wall pegs like tired birds.

"This little girl sure makes a lot of money being a dancer," Wynn's mother says. "I guess she's auditioning in private for a musical."

"They have to take their clothes off in musicals these days, or else nobody comes," Wynn's father says.

At the conclusion of the movie, the blond girl is rescued by a policeman who has been masquerading as a pimp.

"I don't think I understood that picture," Wynn's mother says. She's collecting the empty cups. "Did you understand it?" she asks her husband.

"Of course I did," Wynn's father says.

"Let me do that," Annalee says. She takes the cups out to the kitchen.

"I'd like to punch her boyfriend in the nose," Wynn's mother whispers.

Wynn is jerking the arm of the sofa back and forth. "This is loose," he tells her. "Remind me next time. Make a list, and I'll do everything at once."

"I can take care of that," Wynn's father says. "I'm going to get up early and take care of everything first thing in the morning."

At the trailer park, Annalee and Wynn sit on the hood of Wynn's truck and look at the sky. Wynn knows a lot about the universe; he knows that all stars lead similar lives except in the manner of their deaths. He understands how it is that some of the stars are no longer suns but the light from suns that existed thousands of years ago, and he knows that if it were possible to travel at the speed of light you'd never die.

"A girl I know saw Rodney with someone else," Annalee says.

"You should get out of Dixon," Wynn says. "People shouldn't spend all their lives in one place."

"Dixon's all right," Annalee says.

There is piano music coming from the trailer just east of Wynn's. It's Gus J. Fouts playing "One for My Baby." He plays Thursdays through Sundays at the Holiday Inn, and for his neighbors the rest of the time.

"Do you think people can love you and hurt you at the same time?" Annalee asks.

Wynn is squinting at a plane moving north. "Not over and over again."

Annalee nods her head. She's watching the highway for her boyfriend's headlights, which will be moving fast and turning suddenly.

"There are men who would die before they'd hurt you," Wynn says.

Annalee looks in the direction of the music in order to keep her face out of Wynn's sight. "One for My Baby" has blended into "Stormy Weather," and she begins to cry.

After midnight, through his closed windows, Wynn can hear Gus J. Fouts playing. Sometimes it makes him mad; sometimes he thinks he would be lonely without it. It's not like a radio—he can't turn it on or off—but something valuable happens. It's as though emotions forming in the atmosphere were making their way into his body like oxygen. They make his life real to him. He throws off his clothes and lies on his bed, so that he can be asleep before the music stops.

Prisoners of Love

Last year, when I was twelve years old, my mother married her pen pal, Bennett Jensen, who was in the Wyoming State Penitentiary for holding up a gas station. She had gotten Bennett's name from an ad in the newspaper. He and my mother got married in the warden's office on a Friday morning, while I was in school, and on Saturday afternoon I went with her to the prison, which was almost two hours away, in Rawlins. The three of us ate lunch in the visitors' room. My mother had brought sandwiches wrapped in heart-shaped napkins.

"With a little luck, Scott," Bennett said, "I'll be out in four years." He was small and stocky, and had blue eyes and black glasses.

"Four years goes by like nothing," my mother said. "Think of how often we have a new president."

"It will seem faster now that I have a family to come home to," he told her.

We were living in the Medicine Bow Mobile Home Park, next to the Chevrolet dealership where my mother worked as a secretary. I went to the middle school across the highway. I was on the soccer team, and we played schools from all around Laramie and usually won. My father, who was also remarried, sometimes came to the games with his stepson, Gerald, who was eight. We had a game the week after my mother married Bennett. "Tell me what he's like," my father said. He already knew that Bennett was in prison. It was the end of September, and we were walking to the car, after the game, through fallen leaves

"He's nice," I told him. "I don't know him too well."

"I guess he doesn't come over to the trailer much," my father said. He laughed, and Gerald imitated him.

We got in the car and drove to Ted's Pizzeria, near the University of Wyoming, where our team went to celebrate after we played. The sun was going down, and the sky was red in front of us and dark behind us. Gerald was sitting in the front seat, between my father and me, pushing buttons on the radio. "Quit," my father told him.

"Yes, sir," Gerald said. My father was six-four and weighed two hundred and fifty pounds. He was the assistant principal at Gerald's school.

At Ted's Pizzeria, my friends on the team—Matt Whaler and Joe Kemp—were sitting at a booth next to the jukebox. They already had their pizza and Cokes. My father and Gerald and I sat at the booth behind them and my father ordered a pepperoni pizza, Cokes for

Gerald and me, and a beer for himself. Most of the parents didn't drink beer after the games, in order to set an example for us, and I was embarrassed that my father didn't know that. He didn't come to the games as often as they did, and he had never volunteered to referee.

"I'm going to play on a Little League softball team next year, Scott," Gerald said. "Dad said I have to." He had a crewcut and was overweight. Until my father married his mother, a year and a half earlier, Gerald had lived in an apartment with his grandmother. My father said Gerald had never done anything there except watch TV and eat cookies.

"Softball's fun," I said. "I used to play, too." As I was listening to Gerald, I was also trying to listen to Joe and Matt's conversation about a girl I knew, describing the things she was supposed to have done with a ninth grader. They were talking quietly, but I heard, "took her bra off," and "on her knees," along with some things I had done with her myself. What they were saying bothered me more than I thought it would.

"You can get to be just as good an athlete as Scott," my father told Gerald. "It's just practice. There's no talent involved, as far as I can see."

"I don't agree with that," I told him. But he had turned away from us, to watch Joe Kemps's mother's backside as she leaned over a table to clean up a spilled drink.

After we ate our pizza, we drove to my father's house—he wanted me to say hello to my stepmother. They lived in a ranch house off the highway, at the foot of the Laramie Range. They had five acres of land and a corral, where they kept two horses. Their dogs, Cody and Belle—two white German shepherds—ran out to greet us. It was dark now, and the moon was rising over the hill in back of their property.

Inside, my stepmother, Linda, took some cookies out of a package and put them on a plate, and we ate these in the kitchen. "So who won?" she asked.

"We did," I told her.

"Isn't that nice," she said.

"Why don't you stay overnight?" Gerald asked me.

"I can't," I told him. "My mother doesn't like to be alone, unless she knows in advance, so she can make other plans." I noticed my stepmother's eyebrows rise. "What she does," I explained, "is make plans to stay with a girlfriend, or have the girlfriend stay at our trailer."

Gerald took me into his room to see his hamsters, and then we went outside to visit the horses. He was supposed to start riding lessons soon. My father taught me, when I was four or five, but Linda was nervous about letting my father put Gerald on a horse. She was afraid he would be too reckless.

Their horses were sorrel mares that looked pale in the moonlight. I climbed the fence and mounted the smaller one bareback. "I'll help you up, if you want," I told Gerald.

"I'm not sure I should," he said.

"Just climb the fence and get on in back of me," I told him. I helped him on and walked the mare around the corral. Gerald had his hands pressed against my back. "She can tell how you feel," I said. "She'll be easier to handle if you can get her confidence."

"I am trying to get her confidence," Gerald said.

"I can tell," I told him. "I'm just trying to tell you

69

about horses in general." We got off and walked back to the house, toward a square of light that was shining through the sliding glass door in their family room. Cody and Belle were playing with us, running in circles around our feet and nipping at our jeans.

"You won't tell my mom I rode the horse, will you?" Gerald asked me.

"Why would I?" I said.

My father took me home at ten o'clock. My mother was waiting for me outside, sitting on the steps of our mobile home. "I was worried about you," she said when I got out of the car. "You usually don't stay at Ted's that long."

"Dad took me to his house afterward," I told her.

"I bet that was fun for you," she said. "I know you like those dogs." We went inside and took off our jackets. It had gotten cool out.

"I'd still like to get one of my own," I told her.

"I know you would, honey," she said, "but all anyone has here, in the mobile home park, are chihuahuas and miniature poodles. And they're locked up all day in these little trailers." She brushed some dirt off my jeans. "When Bennett gets out," she told me, "we'll move into a house like Dad's and get a German shepherd. Bennett mentioned in his last letter that he'd also like to have a swimming pool."

"What kind of job will Bennett have when he gets out?" I asked.

"I don't know exactly," she said, "but I think he has some automotive skills. He might work in a service station, fixing cars." She sat on the floor and unlaced her tennis shoes. "Well, maybe not in a service station.

Maybe at the dealership where I work. The swimming pool may be a little unrealistic," she added.

On Saturday, while my mother was visiting Bennett, I walked to the mall to meet Matt, and we each spent fifteen dollars on a video game called Rancho Deluxe. The object was to make the little cowboys rope horses that galloped in from both sides of the screen, while helicopters tried to shoot them down with lasers.

Afterward, we walked through the stores, looking for girls we knew. Matt's girlfriend had broken up with him a few days earlier. "You're not looking for anyone in particular, either, are you?" he asked me.

"Not at all," I told him. "Just anyone good-looking."

"I know what you mean," he said. We stopped in front of a shoe store, to look at a pair of black cowboy boots with silver trim along the sides and outlining the tops. "There aren't many girls worth really liking," Matt said. "Mostly, they're a lot of trouble."

"I know that," I told him.

"That's why it's better to see more than one at a time," he said. "If you start to like someone too much, you can switch to the other girl, and go back and forth like that."

"It might even be safer to have three," I told him.

We walked on past the shoe store and into Mc-Donald's, and ordered Cokes. "I guess that at some time," Matt said, when we sat down, "like when you want to get married, you have to narrow down your choices to one. Or else just get someone pregnant."

"That's probably the easiest way to decide," I told him.

It was six o'clock when I got home, and I cleared off the table and got out the plates and silverware. My mother came home a few minutes later. "How was your day, honey?" she asked me.

"Okay," I told her. "How was yours?"

Without answering, she took a dish of meatloaf and mashed potatoes out of the refrigerator and put it into the cabinet that held our pots and pans. Then she realized her mistake and put it in the microwave. "My mind is on Bennett," she said. "I was thinking about him, in his cell, being unhappy, and how he could be here with us. I was thinking about what a long time four years is." We sat down to eat dinner. I had been invited to a party that night, which I wanted to go to, but when I mentioned it to my mother, she said, "I had planned on an evening with just the two of us, Scott. I thought we could make popcorn and watch TV."

"I can't stay home with you all the time," I told her.

"I know," she said. "But it would mean a lot to me tonight." We washed the dishes and went into the living room. My mother put on her glasses and turned on a movie about a serial killer.

"What's wrong?" I asked her, halfway through. I had noticed she had tears on her face.

"Look at how they portray criminals on television," she said. "Like they're not even human beings."

"But this man killed a lot of people," I told her.

"That doesn't mean he's not a person," my mother said, "or that he doesn't have feelings." She stood up and went into her bedroom to change into her nightgown and robe. While she was gone, I called the house where the party was taking place and asked to speak with the girl Joe and Matt had talked about.

"I haven't seen you in a while," I said. "I just wondered how you were."

"Why don't you come over and find out?" she asked me.

"I can't," I told her. "I'd like to, though." My mother came back into the room, and we watched the rest of the movie. I had a hard time paying attention. I was worrying about who else might be at the party and daydreaming about what I might be doing if I were there.

My father called the next morning, to say that he wanted to take me to a livestock auction. He didn't want any livestock, himself, but he liked to guess the animals' weights and what they sold for. He said that Gerald was staying home, this time.

After the auction, we went to a steakhouse on the road to Horse Creek. My father took off his cowboy hat and set it on an empty chair. "Order anything on the menu," he told me.

"Why?" I asked.

"Because I said so." When I couldn't make up my mind right away, he ordered for me—the largest steak and an extra order of onion rings. We spoke about cattle until the food came, and then he said, "I thought you might want to talk about Bennett Jensen, Scott. It would be good for you to get it off your chest."

"I don't have anything to say about Bennett," I told him.

"Aren't your friends giving you a hard time about

the thing prisons have now," he asked me, "where the married convicts can spend time alone with their wives?"

"My friends don't know yet about Bennett," I told him. "And anyway, I don't know what you're talking about."

"I'm asking you if your mother had a honeymoon night with Bennett Jensen," he said.

"No," I told him. "At least not that I know of."

"Is that right?" my father said. He ate the last bite of his steak, and, without asking, cut off a small piece from mine and put it on his plate. "The reason I wanted to know, Scott, is I was worried about your mother being alone with Mr. Jensen. I'm sure you are, too."

"Not really," I said. "If you met him on the street, you wouldn't guess he was a criminal."

"What do you mean, 'If you met him on the street'?" my father said. "Is he getting out early?"

"No," I told him. "I meant, if you saw him in prison, you'd know he'd done something wrong, but only because he was in jail."

"I see," my father said. "Okay, then." He whistled for the waitress and paid the bill, and we walked outside and got in the car.

"Are we going to your house, to see Linda and Gerald?" I asked.

"Who?" my father said. "Oh. No, not today." He drove in the direction of the mobile home park and stopped at a bar a few blocks before it. I waited for him outside, on the sidewalk. It was almost hot out, and I stood in the shade of the neon sign. He came out carrying a paper sack. "I bought a wedding present for your mother," he told me.

She was cleaning the trailer, wearing old clothes, and when my father walked in behind me, she went into her bedroom and changed into a blouse and skirt. "Do you know what I was thinking about the other day?" he said, when she came out of her room. He was opening her present, which was a bottle of his favorite whiskey, Black Velvet. "That trip we took to Deadwood, South Dakota." We had gone there when I was seven, to see the graves of Calamity Jane and Wild Bill Hickok.

"What made you think of that?" my mother asked him.

"A book I was reading," he told her, "called *Outlaws and the Women Who Loved Them.*"

"Was the book about particular couples," my mother asked, "or was it making general statements? Because I don't believe you can put women in categories like that."

"Of course you can't," my father said. "That goes without saying." He suggested that I go outside to ride my dirt bike, since the weather was so nice. "Take your time and get some exercise," he told me. "I'll take care of your mother."

I stayed out all afternoon, and when I came home, it was almost dark. My mother was in the living room, waiting to talk to me. She hadn't started to make dinner yet. "Sit down and listen to me," she said. "Dad is thinking about coming back to us. We talked for a long time, and he made me see some things. For example, he helped me understand why Bennett wanted to marry me. What did he have going for him before he met me? Absolutely nothing. Besides that, he's a criminal."

"Well, you already knew that," I told her.

"I know I did," she said. "But I didn't think of it as such a bad thing." She closed the curtains and heated up soup for dinner, which we ate without talking. I was thinking about where we would live, if my father came back, and who would end up with his dogs and horses, and what would happen to Gerald. My mother was crumbling crackers into her soup. She had already taken off her wedding ring, and it was on the table, next to the bottle of Black Velvet my father had bought. "I think Dad loved me all along," she said. "I think he was just waiting for the right time to tell me."

"Like right after you married somebody else?" I asked.

"That was just bad timing," she told me. "It was an unfortunate coincidence."

"Are you going to come in with me?" I asked her on Saturday, as she was driving me to Rawlins so that Bennett and I could say good-bye. He had written me two letters, before my mother decided to get a divorce, and he had sent me a football he had ordered from a catalogue. My mother and I had just passed the STATE PENITENTIARY. DO NOT PICK UP HITCHHIKERS sign.

"I don't think that would be a good idea," she said.

I went in by myself, and Bennett and I sat at a table in a corner, under the clock. He kept looking at the door, expecting my mother to walk in. "I'm sorry we didn't get to know each other very well, Scott," he said. "I wanted you to have a dog someday, and all the other things you want."

"I know that," I told him.

"Now I don't care if I live or die," he said.

"Maybe you can find another woman to write letters to," I told him.

"I don't think I'll ever care for anyone else the way I care for your mother." He was looking down at the table. His hair was ruffled up from the way he had been running his fingers through it, and he stood up and shook my hand and disappeared through the steel door. I went outside and got in the car.

"How did it go?" my mother asked me. "How upset was he?"

"He was sad," I said. "He was almost crying."

She looked out the window at the prison. There was a cyclone fence all the way around the parking lot, and the way the sun was slanting made the top of it look shiny and sharp, like a knife blade. On the other side of the fence, there was a cemetery with probably a hundred rows of gravestones. "Well, I don't think he'll be much lonelier than he was before he met me," she said. "Do you?"

"Sure," I told her. "But probably not too much," I said, when I saw the look on her face.

We drove back to Laramie, and my father came over soon after we got home. He was wearing a black Western shirt and a new pair of jeans. He sat down on the couch and refused the glass of iced tea my mother offered him. "Linda and I have decided to see a marriage counselor," he told us. "You can't let something as important as a marriage just fall apart. You should be able to work out your problems."

"You're joking," my mother said.

My father was looking at me. "I'm sorry, Scott," he said. "I guess I was confused about my feelings." My mother stood up and went into her bedroom.

After he left, I knocked at her door and went in. She was sitting on her bed, looking out the window and watching my father drive out of our mobile home park. I sat down next to her and she put her arm around me. It was thundering outside, from a long distance away, but it hadn't rained. You could still see a few stars, and the moonlight was shining down through the trees. "Your father shouldn't go around talking about love when he doesn't mean it," she said. "It's not fair. It's like he doesn't realize how serious it is."

We went into the living room to watch TV. My mother chose *Gnaw: Food of the Gods II*. "A horror movie about giant rats," she read out loud from the *TV Guide*. It was still clear outside at midnight, when the movie was over, and we took a walk through the trailer park. No one else was awake, except people's dogs, and by the time we got back to our trailer, they were all barking and trying to get out through the screens.

Reception

My sister, Leslie, got married on a Saturday in March at our church, St. Mary of the Angels, in Glendale. I was the best man for her fiancé because he didn't have any brothers, and so I didn't see my friend Martin Campbell until we were at the reception, which was held in a large room at a resort in the desert, outside of Sun City. Martin had come with his sister and his parents, even though his parents were getting a divorce. The four of them were sitting at a table near the window. "Eric, would you like to sit with us?" Martin's mother, Kay, said. "We have two extra places. Why don't you go check with your mom?"

"She already said it was okay," I told her. I had been expected to sit at the head table, but my father said I'd already been tortured enough, meaning the blue ruffled shirt they had made me wear.

I sat between Martin and his sister, Paula, who was seventeen. She was tall and slender, and had green eyes and light brown hair. She had dropped out of high school recently, and what she hoped to do was move to Los Angeles sometime and become an actress. For the time being, though, she was working at a Burger King. "You almost look like a grown-up," she said to me. "I've never seen you dressed up before."

"Really?" I said. "I get dressed up like this all the time." Martin and I picked up the silverware and tried to balance the knives between the prongs of the forks. We were in our last year at Clear Mountain Middle School, although Martin wasn't sure he'd be able to finish out the year there. It depended on when they sold their house, and where he and his mother and Paula moved to. They lived across the street from us; Martin's father had already moved into an apartment.

The food came—chicken with a sauce, green beans, and twice-baked potatoes. I could see Leslie, at the head table, smiling at Steve, her new husband, and eating a bite of food now and then. She was twenty-two. She was finished with college and was working at a center for handicapped people. Steve was her boyfriend from high school, who worked now for his father's construction company. He was thin and had a dark moustache. He kept one arm around her as he ate his dinner.

"The sauce is the best part," Martin's father said. Martin was scraping it off his chicken.

"Tell your father to let you eat what you want," Kay said.

"Let me eat what I want," Martin told his father.

"Who's stopping him?" his father said to Kay.

Our neighbors, the Hanleys, who were sitting at the

next table, began a discussion about real estate prices in our neighborhood, which both of Martin's parents listened to carefully.

Father Hyles, the priest at our church, walked past our table and stood behind my chair for a moment. When he seemed to have everyone's attention, he said, "Weddings are what I like best about being a priest. Baptisms are my second favorite."

"I bet sermons and funerals are far down on the list," Martin's father said.

"Another totally inappropriate comment," Kay said, as soon as Father Hyles was out of hearing.

After our plates were cleared away, the tables were pushed back and the band my parents had hired set up its equipment. The room we were in had a sliding glass door that opened onto a patio, and Martin and I went out there and sat in uncomfortable white wire chairs. "Doesn't your father like priests?" I asked Martin.

"He doesn't believe in religion," Martin said. "He thinks it makes people stupid." He took off his suit jacket, folded it carefully, and laid it across a small, round table. It was six o'clock. The sun had already set behind a plateau we could see far off in the distance, but it was still light. The desert looked like a pool of gold water. The subdivision Martin and I lived in, which was near Paradise Valley, was new when we first lived there, and we could walk out of our yards and into the desert. Now the subdivision was built up so much that it was just large houses and green lawns as far as you could see.

"For an Apache runner," Martin said, "like two hundred years ago, it would be nothing for him to run that far and back again." He was pointing to the plateau, which, because of the sunset, looked as though there were a fire burning behind it. "He might be on his way to find peyote in Mexico," he told me. "I think the first Indians to use it were Apaches, around 1870 or so."

"What is peyote supposed to be like?" I asked him.

"I read that it's like looking through a kaleidoscope, only seeing something holy," he said. "Or being able to look into the future."

Paula appeared at the door and smiled at us. She was wearing a red dress that was off the shoulders a little. "You found a nice place to escape to," she said.

"I know we did," I told her.

"It's too hot in there," Martin said.

"There's a lot of champagne, though, and they're not checking I.D.'s," Paula said. "Well, I guess they'd probably check yours," she added. She walked over to a marble birdbath, in the center of the patio. "If this were my wedding," she said, "I'd have a big fountain of champagne right here, where everyone could fill their glasses. And I'd have a limousine to take my husband and me to our new house."

"Right," Martin said.

"That's probably no stupider than the things you wish for," she told him.

It was getting cool outside, and after she left, Martin put his jacket back on and pulled down his shirt cuffs. "Some of the waitresses here are cute," he said. "I like the one with the black hair."

"She's at least eighteen," I told him.

"She's also about six feet tall," he said. Both of us were on the small side—not unusually small, but there were boys in our class who were already as tall as they would probably get. They were the assholes, for the most part.

From inside, we could hear the band playing its first song—the theme music from *The Godfather*. We stood up and moved close enough to the sliding glass door to be able to watch without seeing our own reflections. First Leslie and Steve danced, and then Leslie and my father danced. My father was not a very emotional person, and I was surprised to see the expression on his face as he danced with her. I noticed my mother standing next to the photographer, motioning for him to take pictures.

"Leslie looks good," Martin said. The regular lights had been turned down, and there were colored lights softly flashing around the room, turning Leslie's dress and the flowers in her hair pink, and green, and pale yellow. The train of her dress swished on the floor, around her high heels, like a white sheet curling up in the wind. My father managed not to step on it.

When it was dark outside, Martin and I went back in. The cake had already been cut, and we each had a piece. Almost everyone was dancing, including Martin's parents, although they weren't dancing with each other. They were dancing with the Hanleys. In between songs they switched partners and danced with our other neighbors, the Beckwiths. Then they sat down at a table with Martin and me, one on each side of us.

Paula walked up to me. "Do you want to dance?" she said. "Or would you rather just sit here all night, looking bored?" She took my arm and we danced to "Someone to Watch Over Me." In her high heels she was taller than I was, and she kicked them off and put her head on my shoulder.

"What are you doing?" I asked her.

"I'm drunk," she told me. "I have to lean against people." She was talking right into my ear. "Look at your parents dancing," she said.

My mother had her arms around my father's neck, and his hands were low on her back. The two of them were hardly moving. "That's so nice," Paula said.

"They don't normally dance like that," I told her. "But they took a ballroom dancing class, and now they're more interested in it."

"You don't learn to dance like that in a class," Paula said. "You dance like that when you can't wait to go home and go to bed with each other."

"That's hard to imagine," I told her. "I mean, since they're my parents."

"You dance like that when you're happy," she said. I could feel her tears wetting my shirt.

The song ended, and I asked, "Would you like to dance with me again? At least until you feel better?"

"I don't think so," she said. "I just wanted to see what it would be like, the one time." She walked away from me, toward the restroom. I stood in a corner of the room and saw Martin standing near the refreshments, talking to a waitress who was pouring punch into glass cups. She wasn't the black-haired one; she was a short, thin girl with reddish hair, who looked young. With hardly any surprise, I watched Martin touch her hair. Maybe she'll dance with him, I thought. But then I remembered that wouldn't be allowed—for her to dance at a wedding when she was supposed to be working.

By the end of the evening, everyone in my family looked tired. Leslie and Steve were supposed to leave soon. They were spending the night at a hotel near the airport, and in the morning they were going to fly to San Francisco for their honeymoon. Before our priest left he had taken them aside, as my family was saying good-bye to him, and said a prayer. "May the blessing of Almighty God, the Father, and the Son descend upon you, grace your marriage, and remain forever."

"Amen," we all said.

Now my mother and Leslie were sitting alone at a table in the back of the room. A lot of people had already left. I was standing on the dance floor with Steve. He was wearing Leslie's garter on his wrist. "I hope all the pictures turn out okay," he said. "I wish we had video-taped everything. Wouldn't it have been nice for Leslie and me to watch when we're old?"

Behind us, the band was taking apart its equipment. My father was leaning against the wall, talking to the resort manager. It looked as though he was thanking him for doing a good job.

My family and Martin's family left at the same time. We said good-bye to Leslie and Steve and watched them drive away. Martin said, "I wish I were flying to some-place like San Francisco tomorrow."

"Well, maybe that's where we'll end up, honey," Kay said.

"I didn't mean it that way," Martin said quickly. "I meant, for a vacation." He walked away from us, to the edge of the parking lot and a few steps out into the desert. The night sky was bright, because the stars were out, but there wasn't any moonlight.

"Martin," his father said loudly.

"Don't yell at him, for Pete's sake," Kay said. "Does it make sense to shout at him because he's upset?"

"No," Martin's father said. "It makes sense to let him do what he wants when he's upset."

Martin was already on his way back, walking in a large half-circle to avoid his parents. "Do you want to ride with the Campbells?" my mother asked me. Martin was starting to get into the back seat of his father's car, and when he heard my mother's question he got out in order to let me in first. But I said, No, and he got into the car, next to Paula, and his parents got in the front seat, and they drove out of the parking lot and onto the highway.

Looking for Love

The only person Jodi Horton wants to invite to her high school graduation party is Eduardo Espada, an illegal alien who works at the gas station near the high school. "That's it?" her stepfather, Lowell, asks. "What about girlfriends from school? What about some of the neighbor kids?" He and Jodi and Jodi's son, Duane, are sitting in the kitchen, having breakfast.

"You mean girlfriend, and she's busy," Jodi says. "I was going to invite the 'Miami Vice' cast, but I was pretty sure they wouldn't come."

"You can even invite teachers, if you want," Lowell tells her. "When I was your age, teachers were the guests of honor at graduation parties."

"Teachers," Jodi says. "Oh, sure." She picks up Duane and carries him into the bedroom to get him dressed. She had Duane when she was fifteen, a year before her mother died in a drowning accident at Mission Beach. Duane's father, an ex-classmate of Jodi's, moved away before the baby was born. Jodi had been too embarrassed to tell him she was pregnant. Jodi's grandmother—her mother's mother—looks after Duane on weekdays, while she is in school.

A little after eight, Lowell drops Duane off at Jodi's grandmother's apartment and then drives Jodi to school. She makes him drive around the block past the gas station. "There he is," she says. "He's eating something and reading a magazine."

"I could use some gas," Lowell says.

"Get it someplace else, then, because I don't want him to think I spend my life following him around," Jodi tells him.

After Lowell drops her off in front of the school, he doubles back and drives up to the full-service island. He gets out of the car and watches as Eduardo checks the oil and fills the gas tank. Eduardo is twenty-two or twenty-three, Lowell figures. As far as he knows, Jodi has never had a real date with Eduardo; he's just met her at the mall a few times, and at San Luis Park.

"Sixteen dollars," Eduardo says.

"Fine. Thanks," Lowell says. He starts the car and lets it idle a couple of minutes while Eduardo waits on another customer, then he pulls out and drives to Sears, where he's the appliance sales manager.

In the evening, Lowell and Jodi attend a service for all the high school graduates at Jodi's mother's church. It had once been Unitarian, but before Jodi's mother joined it had been changed and renamed by its members the Church of Innate Goodness and moved to the basement of a Howard Johnson's. After the service, during the refreshment hour, Jodi and Lowell stand outside, on the sidewalk in front of the motel sign, so that Lowell can smoke. "I think some of your mother's friends wanted to talk to you," Lowell says.

"Well, I can't stand how nice everyone is in there," Jodi tells him. "I can't tell what anyone is really thinking, and I can't swallow this crap about people being so wonderful."

"I think they're just saying that people could be wonderful," Lowell says. He lights another cigarette and takes his wallet out of his back pocket. He shows Jodi his high school graduation picture. "This was taken thirty years ago, so don't laugh," he tells her. "This is how everyone looked back then."

"That's pretty hard to believe," Jodi says. She takes out her own wallet and shows Lowell pictures of some of the kids in her homeroom. "They're not exactly friends," she says. "They're just people I've seen around a lot for the past four years."

On the way home, they stop at Jodi's grandmother's apartment to pick up Duane. He's asleep on her bed, and Jodi's grandmother, in a flowered housedress, is in the living room with Jodi's uncle, Phil. He hugs Jodi. "Congratulations, honey," he says. "Good for you." He sits back down and runs his hands over his face.

"Phil lost his cat today," Jodi's grandmother tells them. "His neighbor ran her over in the driveway."

"Why did he do that?" Jodi says.

"Because he didn't see her, I hope," Phil says. "He offered to pay me, so I told him to try and put a price on the head of his best friend." He walks over to the air conditioner and puts his hand in front of the vent. He's small and thin and is wearing striped work overalls.

"What the hell is wrong with this thing?" he shouts. "I thought you just paid through the nose to get it fixed!"

"Duane is sleeping, dear," Jodi's grandmother says.

"I'm sorry," Phil tells her. He sits down on the couch and then stands up again. "I could use a drink. How about a drink, Lowell? Mom? How about a drink?"

"You have one," Lowell says.

"I'm being a terrible hostess," Jodi's grandmother says. She walks into the kitchen and comes back with Phil's drink, a plate of cookies, and a pamphlet about a secretarial school, which she hands to Jodi. "I'd love to see you give this a try," she tells her. "I can picture you behind the desk in a dentist's office."

"Beth Ann really wanted her to go to college," Lowell says. "I went to junior college about a hundred years ago."

"Do you know what school I went to?" Phil asks them.

"The school of life," Jodi and Lowell say.

"Okay. That's right," Phil says.

Jodi places the pamphlet on her grandmother's coffee table. "Eduardo Espada and I will get married, and I'll get a job someplace and have more kids," she tells her grandmother.

The day of the graduation party is cloudy and hot. Jodi's uncle mows the lawn and trims around the edges with a Weed Eater; Lowell and Jodi's grandmother set up a long table in the back yard and hang multicolored balloons in the fruit trees. They make a big banner that says CONGRATULATIONS JODI HORTON! and tack it to the house along the trim above the sliding glass door. Then they put out bowls of chips and Mexican hot sauce.

"How do I look?" Jodi asks. She comes outside wearing a sleeveless pink dress and white high heels. "I think the dress makes me look a little thinner."

"You look great," Lowell tells her.

"Well, I know I don't look great, but thank you anyway," Jodi says. "I mean, thanks, even if you're lying."

"I'm not lying," Lowell says.

"You wouldn't tell the truth if it hurt someone's feelings, though," Jodi tells him. "Not like some jerks I know."

"How do you always know such terrible people?" Jodi's grandmother says. "All your mother wanted was for you to be around people who loved you."

"I went on to high school," Jodi says.

The guests begin to arrive at four o'clock—two of Jodi's grandmother's friends, the next-door neighbors and a couple from across the street, and three of Lowell's coworkers at Sears. Eduardo shows up late with three candy bars for Duane. He shakes hands with Lowell and puts his arm around Jodi. He's handsome and compact— slightly shorter and thinner than she is.

"Thanks a lot for coming," Jodi tells him. "I was afraid you'd forget or feel weird or something."

"I have the day off anyway," Eduardo says.

Lowell plays tapes on Jodi's portable stereo, and then he brings out his camera and takes pictures. For one of the pictures, Jodi and Eduardo stand on either side of the birdhouse Jodi made in shop. It's three stories tall, each level smaller than the one beneath it. Each story has several carefully cut, round holes. Jodi spent hours after school working on it. She received an A for the semester.

Jodi's grandmother passes around the high school yearbook for everyone to sign. Phil leaves the party for fifteen minutes and comes back with a wicker basket covered with a towel.

"This is for you and Duane both," he tells Jodi. "I have her sister. I drove over to the pound yesterday and picked them out."

"This is really cool," Jodi says. She picks up the cat and kneels down to show it to Duane. "It's really a great present, Uncle Phil."

Jodi's uncle fastens a red plastic collar around the cat's neck. The collar has little bells on it. "This way," he says, "if you keep your ears open, you can keep track of her every second."

By nine o'clock, it's almost dark, and all the guests have left. Duane has fallen asleep on a blanket in the yard, and the paper banner has ripped and is snapping in the wind. Jodi puts Duane to bed and changes into jeans and a T-shirt. "I'm going out," she tells her grandmother and Lowell, who are in the kitchen, putting away food. "There are about fifteen parties going on. Of course, I'm not invited to them, but I think it will be okay if I just show up."

"I thought you said Eduardo was taking you to a movie," Lowell says.

Jodi picks up a container of plastic wrap and slides out five or six inches, slowly pulling it against the serrated edge so that it stretches instead of cuts. "Well, he was talking about wanting to see *Friday the 13th—Part VI.*"

Lowell makes coffee, and he and Jodi's grandmother take their cups into the den. Jodi's grandmother holds the cat on her lap and watches television, and Lowell leafs through a newsletter called *Looking for Love*. It was how he had met Jodi's mother, ten years earlier. "What if I had never answered her ad?" Lowell says. "Or what if she hadn't bothered calling me?"

"You wouldn't be going through all this heartache now," Jodi's grandmother says.

At eleven-thirty, when Lowell is in bed but still awake, he hears Jodi unlocking the front door. He listens to her walk down the hall and hears water running in the bathroom. He gets up to talk to her. He knows that nothing he says will make the slightest difference—what does he know about love except how much it matters?

The Nevada School of Acting

Yesterday, at the laundromat, a man I didn't know asked me to wash his clothes.

"Maybe he thought you worked there," my mother, Val, says.

"No, he didn't," I tell Val. We're talking about this while we're eating lunch with my brother Sonny and his girlfriend, Irene. Sonny just got out of the Southern Nevada Correctional Center—he was in for six months for robbing a supermarket.

"He could have thought you were someone else, Sherri, or maybe he was crazy," Irene says. "Maybe he asks people to wash his clothes all the time."

"Has anyone ever asked you that?" I say.

"Only Sonny," Irene says.

"Sweetheart," Val says, "this isn't something to cry about, is it?"

I blow my nose into my napkin. I'm embarrassed to be crying in front of Sonny and Irene. "I'd just like to know what it is about my looks that makes strangers think I'd do their laundry," I say.

My mother puts her arm around me. She is a normal-sized person, and I weigh eighty-two pounds. "I developed late, too," Val tells me, "but I survived it. I studied hard in school and waited for my body to change, and then I got married."

"I studied hard in school and then I got into trouble," Sonny says.

Val takes off her glasses and looks at him. "Sometime I'd like to pin you down on this, Sonny," she says, "and find out what went wrong."

"Somebody called the police," Sonny says.

After lunch, Val drives into Winston to buy groceries, and I calm down and read a book called *Superstar Make-Overs*. I've just started high school, and there are all those imitation movie stars walking around the hallways. I try not to say or do anything that would seem bizarre on, for example, "Dynasty," so that I will fit in. There is a boy I like who is good-looking enough to be a rock star.

I'm in the kitchen thinking about this boy when my stepfather, Richard, drives up. He has a drink with him, in a plastic cup, and he sits on the hood of his car, drinking and looking out at the desert. He lets his moccasins slide off his feet. He drinks too much, which Val says is because he's unhappy. I tap on the window to get his attention, and he waves to me slowly, as though he's under water. He comes into the house and watches a "Leave It to Beaver" rerun with Sonny, Irene, and me.

"I'd like for us to have a house just like theirs," Irene tells Sonny, "only with a hot tub in the back yard."

"And without Eddie Haskell," Sonny says. "I met enough Eddie Haskells oiling around in prison."

"Eddie Haskell never went to prison. What are you talking about?" Richard says. "I bet you're thinking of 'The FBI.' "

"I'm just thinking of real life," Sonny says.

When the program is over, Irene and I go into the bathroom with her makeup kit.

"I'd like to try this mauve eye-shadow on you," Irene says. "It will look great."

"I don't expect to look beautiful," I tell her. "I just don't want to stand out as being extra ugly."

Sonny is sitting on the edge of the bathtub to keep us company, reading the want ads. "Here's a job for a security guard at a bank," he says. "I guess they wouldn't want me."

"The trick is to look good without anyone knowing that you care so much about looking good," Irene tells me.

"Let me ask a question," I say. "Is there anything you can care about that is okay for people to know you care about?"

"Not in high school," Irene says. "Except for maybe Bruce Springsteen."

She is doing something to my hair to make it stand out from my head in all directions like antennae. "This will give you more height," she says.

Sonny has put down the paper and is staring at my head.

"What's wrong?" I ask him.

"Well, nothing," Sonny says. I pick up a towel and drape it over my head.

We spend the rest of the afternoon out in the desert with Richard, who is trying to find snakes to shoot with his .22. Sonny holds the gun while Irene, Richard, and I look for snakes. Richard has had too much to drink to hold the gun himself.

"Let's throw darts instead," Sonny tells Richard. "Me and Irene against you and Sherri."

"No, thanks," Richard says. "I'm not in the mood."

"I wish Val would come home," I tell Irene. She and I have just seen a snake and have headed Richard in the opposite direction. He makes a grab for the gun, which throws Sonny off balance for a minute and scares everybody.

"Please don't do that again," Sonny tells him.

"I'm not drunk," Richard says.

"Maybe you're just a little drunk," Sonny says.

"Sherri," Richard says, "do you think I'm drunk?"

"I think I don't want to spend one more second looking at snake holes," I tell him.

Richard shades his eyes and watches a car pass by on the highway.

"That's probably Ward Cleaver, taking his kids to the arcade," Sonny tells Richard, who watches the sand and dust rise on the side of the road until it clears, and then walks home.

.   .   .

In the evening, I'm listening to sixties music in my room and examining my wardrobe when Sonny comes in and sits on the floor.

"I'm really tired," he says. "I forgot how weird things can be in everyday life."

"You had a lot of girlfriends in high school," I tell Sonny. "Did you ever go out with anyone as abnormal as me?"

"I never went out with anyone as normal as you," he says. "I did go out with girls bigger than you, if that's what you mean, but that was just by accident."

The phone rings, and it's for me. I take it in Val and Richard's bedroom, and then go back to my own room.

"Who was that?" Sonny says.

"Kim Kosky, Luann Hoblitzel, and Reenie Shaughnessy—girls from school. They wanted to know why I'm so ugly."

"Come on," Sonny says.

"You don't make this kind of stuff up, Sonny. They said, 'Why don't you have dates?' They call up about once a month. They wait until they think I've forgotten, and then they do it again."

Sonny doesn't say anything.

"They may as well just shoot me," I say.

"Let's drive into town with Irene for some ice cream," Sonny says finally.

The boy I like is walking through downtown Winston with his arm around a girl. I crouch down in the back of Sonny's VW while Irene runs in for the ice-cream cones, and then I make Sonny drive home the long way.

"Maybe you feel like telling us who that person was," Sonny says once we're out of town and I'm off the floor of the car.

"Just this famous movie producer who wants to make me a star," I say, even though I once read in a book that it's important to face up to whatever horrible things are happening to you. The author didn't think that was too much to ask of human beings.

Irene turns on the radio—really loud, because the top is down. We listen to Julio Iglesias and Willie Nelson thank all the women they've loved. In front of us, there are flashes of lightning, and behind us the lights of Winston are slowly beginning to go out. By the time we're home, the lightning is closer and we can hear thunder. Richard has passed out on the couch, and Val is removing his shoes and socks. I go outside to help Sonny put up the top of his car.

"I bet it's already raining in the mountains," he says.

"What did you act like in prison?" I ask him. "Like everything was all right?"

"Like everything was going to be all right," Sonny says.

Flowers

From inside the back of his van, where he was going through his inventory of silk flowers, Kevin Holt listened to his niece, Nina, talking with Graham Deshablis, who sold paintings on velvet. They were parked at an intersection in Tucson, near the El Con Mall, which was the best place in the city for business. Kevin guessed that Graham was close to his own age—thirty-eight. Nina was thirteen and a half. She helped Kevin after school and on weekends. Nina and Graham had been talking about music, but then they began talking about some events that had been in the paper lately—things having to do with witchcraft and voodoo and murder rituals. "I know somebody who watched an animal sacrifice out in the desert once," Graham said.

"What kind of animal was it?" Nina asked. "And

what do you mean by sacrifice? Do you mean they killed it?"

"It was a dog," Graham said. "They killed it in a strange way—with fire, I think."

Kevin came out of the van then, and Graham walked away to wait on a customer. It was five in the evening on a hot and cloudy Saturday in April. "How did we do?" Kevin asked Nina.

"Seventy-six dollars," she said, "not counting tips. Graham gave me a five-dollar tip, plus he bought me some flowers." She held them up.

"He shouldn't be giving you money, Nina," Kevin said. "That seems weird. And I wish he wouldn't have told you about that dog thing."

"I didn't really understand it anyway," Nina said.

She and Kevin put the folding chairs and the flowers in the van, and they drove to the mall. Instead of getting paid, Nina liked to go to the mall on Saturdays and pick out something for Kevin to buy her. He followed her into a store, and she stopped in front of a rack of short skirts. "What do you think?" she said. "Some of my friends at school have these same skirts."

"I like the blue one," Kevin said. He stood in the back of the store, leaning against the wall, while she tried it on.

"I think I'll get it," Nina said when she came out of the dressing room. "My husband will pay for it," she told the salesperson.

"Why do you say things like that?" Kevin said in the van on the way home. "Why do you try to embarrass me?"

"Because you're so calm all the time, it drives me crazy," she said.

Kevin pulled into the Desert-View Apartments. He shared a first-floor apartment with his sister, Trudy; Nina and her father, Tom, who was Kevin's older brother, lived in a second-floor apartment across the parking lot. Nina's parents were divorced, and Nina's mother was remarried and living in Houston with a man Nina didn't like. She refused to go there, even for a visit, and she wouldn't see her mother in Tucson if her mother's husband came along. All she would say to Kevin about him was that he was "gross" and "stupid," but Kevin had heard her say that about so many people that he couldn't pinpoint what these things meant.

This evening, because Tom had a date, Nina was having dinner with Kevin and Trudy. They ate in the kitchen. The dining room was Trudy's sewing room. She specialized in costumes and bridesmaid's gowns, and she also told fortunes for her customers, as a bonus.

"Don't give me too much," Nina told her aunt. "I'm not hungry. I never feel like eating after I see Graham Deshablis, and not because of anything he tells me," she said, looking at Kevin. "It's because I like him."

"Don't let men interfere with your eating habits," Trudy said. "That's dangerous."

Kevin was pouring Nina a glass of milk. "What do you mean by 'like'?" he asked her. "Graham is as old as I am. I'm sure he likes you, too, Nina, but you're just a kid to him, which is how it should be."

"I was talking about how *I* feel, not about how *he* feels," Nina said.

"What does this person look like?" Trudy asked.

"Kind of like a biker," Nina said, "but cleaner, and sort of gentle."

"He has a big knife he carries around with him in a sheath on his belt," Kevin told Trudy.

"But only for peeling apples and stuff," Nina said.

After dinner, while they were cleaning up the kitchen, they decided to see a movie. Because it was a Saturday night, Nina would only agree to go to a movie theater on the opposite side of Tucson, so that she wouldn't have to chance running into anyone she knew. "Don't take this personally," she said, as they were looking at movie listings in the paper, "but I can't afford to let my friends know that I do anything with my relatives."

Once they had eliminated everything they'd already seen, they were left with "Sorority Slaughter," which Kevin didn't want Nina to see, and so they looked for something else to do. They decided on a church rummage sale they saw advertised, which wasn't too far from where they lived.

" 'Five dollars a bag, 7:30 to 9 P.M.,' " Trudy read. "Let's get moving."

It was seven-twenty when they arrived at the church, and there was a crowd of people—mostly senior citizens—standing on the steps. "When they open the doors," Trudy whispered as they were waiting in line, "just barrel your way in and grab up anything that looks good. We can sort through it later. The important thing is to get to the stuff first, before anyone else. Don't feel sorry for them because they're old."

"Trudy's just kidding," Kevin told Nina.

"No, I'm not," Trudy said.

After the sale—they bought fifteen dollars' worth of household items and clothes and paperbacks—Nina was hungry, and they drove to a pizza place Kevin used to go to with a girlfriend, south of Tucson, off the highway in the desert. It was almost like a truck stop. They sat in a booth and ordered pizza and beer and a Coke for Nina. "This is just the kind of place you'd know about," Nina told Kevin. "You don't feel like you have to be any particular kind of person in here. You can just relax and be anybody. You could probably even be yourself."

"You can do that anywhere, you know," Kevin said.

"Only if you're really cool," Nina said, "or if you're really stupid, or if you're really drunk."

"Getting drunk isn't all it's cracked up to be," Kevin said. "Or do you know that already?"

"I'm not saying," Nina told him.

Trudy was staring at a man who was walking from the rest room to a booth. She was sitting between Kevin and Nina, and she touched their arms. "I think that's Frank North," she said. "We went out once, and he took me to a place where there were pictures of naked women on the walls. It was kind of a club. That was when I decided to start telling fortunes, because when I looked at those creeps and saw what they were underneath they didn't seem so scary. They just seemed lonely."

"What do you see when you look at my face?" Nina asked.

"Somebody really special," Trudy said. "Nina Ann Holt."

"Maybe you need glasses," Nina said.

On the way home, Nina sat in the back, with both of the windows open. They were in Trudy's car, and Kevin was driving. Nina was quiet for so long that Kevin turned around while they were stopped at a red light to see if she was asleep. "What are you thinking about?" he asked her.

"You don't want to know," she said. "Graham Deshablis. You know how you can love someone so much you think you have something when you don't? Well, that's how I feel about him."

"I wish you didn't," Kevin said.

"I don't," Nina told him, "because otherwise I wouldn't have anything. I mean, I don't like anyone else, and I don't want to feel nothing." A few minutes later she slid over in the seat and put her arm out the window. "Somebody in my school killed himself because he felt empty like that."

"How do you know that was why?" Kevin said.

"Because his locker was near mine, and I could see it in his face, like Trudy can. Kevin, watch this in the rearview mirror," she said. "Mom showed me this once when we were driving someplace. Whichever way you tilt your hand is the way your hand will go, because of the force of the air. But if you curve your fingers a little, and keep your hand level, your hand will go up. That's how airplanes work. It's one of those things you think you're not smart enough to understand but then it turns out you are, because they're simple. So if I ever fly anyplace, I'll know what's going on."

"Maybe you'll fly to Houston sometime," Trudy said.

"I don't think so," Nina told her.

At the apartment complex, Nina spotted Tom's girlfriend's car and decided to spend the night at Kevin and Trudy's. "It's not that I don't like her or that I'm mad at Dad," she told them. "I'd just rather stay with you guys." She called her father from the phone in the kitchen, and then she went out on the patio, where her aunt and uncle were sitting. It was eleven-thirty. It was still warm, and the dark sky was overcast; the moon was appearing and disappearing behind the clouds. Two rosebushes that Trudy had planted a few weeks earlier were starting to bloom. There were two small wooden benches on the patio. "I think Dad's feelings are hurt," Nina said. "I don't know what anybody wants from me. No matter what I do, even when I think I'm doing someone a favor, I end up being wrong."

"I'll call your dad and explain it to him," Trudy said. She went inside, and Kevin put his arm around Nina. She was trembling, as though she was trying hard to keep from crying. Then she moved away from him suddenly and kicked over one of the wooden benches, which fell on Trudy's roses. They both leaned over to pick it up, but Kevin reached for it first. If he lifted it up fast enough, he thought, he and Nina might be able to pretend that nothing had happened at all.

Geometry

A week after Denny Long left me to move in with another woman and her two children, my brother-in-law called me at Toys "Я" Us to say that my sister was in labor at South Miami Hospital. I got permission to leave work early, and I drove over and sat in a waiting room with my brother-in-law's family—his mother and stepfather, Vivian and Arthur Banks, and their daughter, Sophia. It was Saturday evening, and except for us the waiting room was empty. We were sitting on green couches.

"How are you managing, honey?" Vivian asked me.

"I'm really lonely," I told her.

"Well, there are plenty of men out there," she said. "Just ask Sophia. Guys are calling her around the clock."

"That's not quite true," Sophia said. "Creeps are calling me around the clock." She was a junior in high school and was doing her geometry homework. She had decorated the cover of her geometry textbook with different kinds of triangles.

Arthur went down to the cafeteria and brought us some sandwiches and Cokes, and, while we ate, Sophia and I talked about her boyfriend, Gus Beekman, who I'd known since eighth grade. He was my age—middle thirties—and he played saxophone with a band that worked at the cheaper Miami Beach hotels. Denny Long managed the band.

"Why is Gus Beekman always the center of conversation in this family?" Vivian said. "Why can't we talk about movies or current events?"

"Because Gus is the coolest person on earth," Sophia said.

When we'd finished eating, Arthur and I collected the garbage and carried it over to the trash can. He was in his work clothes, and he rested his hand on my shoulder. "Is this baby the best thing that has ever happened to us, or am I crazy?" he said.

"I don't think you're crazy at all," I told him.

Charlotte had a baby boy at two-thirty in the morning. My brother-in-law, Barry, came out of the delivery room to tell us. "They shouldn't let people in there," he said. "I've been through hell."

"How is Charlotte?" Vivian and I asked.

"Doing great," Barry said.

I looked at the baby through the glass window of the nursery, and as soon as I got home I called my mother and told her about him. My mother lived in Las Vegas, and when I called she said she had just gotten home from seeing a Wayne Newton show. "That's wonderful, sweetheart," she said. "You and Denny have one now."

"Denny and I split up," I told her. "He moved in with somebody who already has some." She didn't say anything, and I knew that she was feeling bad for me, and for herself because I hadn't told her about this sooner. I changed the subject and talked about the Bankses—about how they had waited at the hospital for the baby to be born, and about how Arthur had brought us all dinner. I talked for five or ten minutes, until my mother said, "Who the hell is Arthur, honey?"

"Arthur Banks," I said. "Your son-in-law's step-father."

"Oh, that's right," my mother said. Then she told me about Wayne Newton, and described his clothes and jewelry.

When I went back to the hospital at noon, Charlotte was wearing the nightgown-and-robe combination our mother had sent. It was red and lacy, and was probably a Frederick's outfit. She was holding the baby. "Would you like to hold him, Beverly?" she asked me.

I picked the baby up and sat with him in a chair by the window. He was twitching and grimacing in his sleep, and was even smaller than I'd imagined he would be. "He's a great baby," I said. "You did a good job, and you must be really happy."

Charlotte put on her glasses. "Happy isn't even the word for it," she said. "I never expected to feel anything like this. I can't explain it, and I can't compare it to anything else. It's one of those things you just have to do before you can know what it's like."

The baby started to fuss. Charlotte asked for him back, and I put him in her arms. He opened his eyes for a few seconds, and it seemed to me as though he already knew who Charlotte was and what he meant to her, and that he could sense how important those things were.

"Did I tell you that Mom called?" Charlotte said. "She went to see Wayne Newton."

"I know," I told her. "I couldn't be more thrilled for her."

Later in the day, I drove to McDonald's with Sophia and Gus, and afterward we went to the beach. We walked out on a pier and sat down and dangled our feet over the edge. Sophia took off her blouse. Underneath, she had on a sleeveless white top. Gus was twisting her hair in his fingers.

"Let's get married and have a baby," Sophia said.

"Maybe when you're a senior," Gus told her. "Have you heard from Denny?" he asked me.

"Of course not," I said. "Why should Denny want to talk to me?"

"I was just asking," he said.

I was thinking about Charlotte and her baby, and about how I should have had a baby when I was nineteen or twenty, the way all of my friends had, instead of waiting for the right situation, which was probably not going to come along until I was too old. "I don't suppose you'd like to have a baby with me, too," I said to Gus.

"Not really." He was lying on his back, looking at the clouds, his head resting on one of Sophia's books. She had brought along homework, but she wasn't doing any of it.

"They're forcing us to go to a pep rally tomorrow at school," Sophia said. "Do you know what a pep rally is?" she asked me.

"Sure," I said.

"Oh." She lay back against Gus's shoulder. "I thought it might be something they just started a few years ago, because it's so stupid. I couldn't believe they had been doing something that stupid for all those years."

Gus and I looked at each other, and I stretched out on the pier and knocked my forehead on the wood.

When we went to see the baby at five o'clock, he was jaundiced and had been put under bright lights in the nursery. We found Vivian and Arthur in Charlotte's room.

"The doctor told us that he's going to be fine," Vivian said. "It's something that happens to newborn babies all the time. It doesn't mean anything terrible— it happened to Barry."

"Did you see him?" Charlotte asked us. She was standing in front of the window in her red robe, looking down at the parking lot. She was running her hands along the dusty venetian blind.

"He looks really pathetic," Sophia said, "especially with that little blindfold on. He looks like some kind of miniature prisoner."

Charlotte burst into tears.

"Thanks for your help," Barry told Sophia.

He went over to Charlotte and put his arms around her. Arthur put his arms around Vivian, and Gus put his arms around Sophia. I sat on the bed and turned on the television. A "Star Trek" rerun was on, and Captain Kirk and Mr. Spock were trapped on a strange planet. Two young women in togas were trying to force them to stay forever.

In the evening, Gus and I drove to a restaurant near my apartment. It had started to rain, and the reflection of the restaurant's green neon sign on the wet pavement made the street look like glass. "What about Sophia?" Gus said. "Do you think she really loves me?"

"I think she'd die for you."

"I know that, Beverly," he said, "but I don't want anyone dying for me. What I want is for a lot of people to love me. I know that's impossible, and I know it's selfish."

"That's called a family," I told him.

Fidelity

Dan Shepherd drove home after work to his new mobile home, which was on a gravel road between the trucking company he owned and a small farm that boarded horses. It was a Friday evening at the end of December. It was raining outside—a steady drizzle that was thawing the ice left on the trees from a recent storm. Dan parked his truck in the yard and brought in his dog, Wander, and then he showered and dressed and drove into Jefferson City to pick up his eleven-year-old son, Ross.

His ex-wife's apartment, where she and Ross had lived for two months, was in a tall brick building in a hilly, decaying neighborhood. The building was called the Jefferson Arms. There were two stone pillars in front, and on each pillar was a small statue of an open-mouthed lion. Dan rode up in the musty elevator to the fifth floor, and ran into his ex-wife, Leigh Ann, in the hallway, putting a bag of trash into the incinerator chute.

"I was just trying to clean up a little," she explained. "No matter what I do, my apartment is always a mess by Friday."

"I know what you mean," he said. She invited him into the apartment and they sat awkwardly together on her pale blue couch. Dan could hear his son's Nintendo game going in the back bedroom. On the coffee table in front of them were stacks of papers from Leigh Ann's high school classes. "It looks like you're keeping busy," he told her.

"In addition to that work," she said, "I'm directing the school play, and we have rehearsals tomorrow. I'm having a problem because all of the girls want to look attractive. They don't care what the parts call for, so long as they can look pretty."

"Is that right?" Dan said.

"Everybody wants to be beautiful," Leigh Ann told him. "It's sad, really. I keep telling them that it's okay to be ordinary, and then I use myself as an example."

"Well, I don't think it's a good one," Dan said.

"Don't you?" Leigh Ann asked. "I thought it was exactly right."

Ross came into the room, then, carrying his overnight bag. He was a small, dark-haired boy, with sharp features. "Don't forget to feed my fish," he told his mother. "Just a little bit in the morning." He put on his glasses and stepped back when Leigh Ann tried to kiss him.

Dan and his son parked in the lot of St. Anne's Hospital and went into the gift shop to buy a deck of cards. Dan's

father had been in the hospital for five weeks, with cancer, and on the way up in the elevator Dan said, "He
looks worse than he did last week, Ross. Don't expect
much."

"I've got two new tricks to show him, if he's
awake," Ross said. "I don't think he'll be able to figure
them out."

The hospital overlooked the Missouri River. The
curtains were open in his father's room, and Dan could
see the dark gleam of the water. His mother was sitting
next to his father's bed, and she put down her magazine
and touched his father's shoulder. "Your favorite person
is here, Andy," she said.

Dan's father raised his head. "Mr. Wizard," he said.

"I know two new ones," Ross told him. He went
out into the hall and came back with an empty food
tray. He put it on the bed, next to his grandfather, and
laid out the cards. "Choose one," he told him. "Just
point to it and I'll show it to you." Dan's father pointed
to the one closest to Ross's left hand, and Ross held it
up to his grandfather's face. "Okay," he said. "Remember it." He picked up the cards, shuffled them, and held
out the deck to Dan. "Do it for him," he told his father.
"Pick up the first one and show it to Grandpa." Dan
did as he was told. "That's it, right?" Ross said. "It's
the card you pointed to?"

"It might be," Dan's father said.

"It is," Ross told him. "I can tell by the look on
your face."

"Come over here and show me how you do that,"
Dan said.

"I'll show you some other time," Ross told him. "I
want Grandpa to see my other trick." But Dan's father

had his eyes closed, and Ross carefully took the tray off the bed and set it on the floor.

Dan and his mother were looking out the window at the street below. "They've taken down all the Christmas lights," Dan said. "I think it's a good thing. They're wasteful."

"They were pretty, though," his mother said. "It was like looking down at a sky full of stars."

"Do you feel like waking up yet, Grandpa?" Ross asked. He was standing next to the bed, holding his cards.

"He'll probably sleep all night," Dan's mother said. "Come back in the morning, Ross. That's when he's alert."

Dan took Ross out for pizza. It was nine-thirty, and the restaurant was filled with noisy teenagers. Their order was taken by a tall, gum-chewing waitress. "You don't really want anchovies, do you?" she said, after Dan ordered.

"Let's see," Dan said. "I ordered them, right? So I guess I want them."

"I can't believe anyone would eat an anchovy," she said. She smiled at him and then at Ross, who looked down at his hands. After she left, Ross excused himself, and Dan watched him walk past a group of laughing girls at the salad bar before he turned down the hall to the restroom.

When he came back, Dan said, "In a few years, you'll be here with your friends."

Ross was looking at a blond-haired girl in a red coat, who was standing near the door with her arms around her boyfriend. "I know that girl," he said. "She's in one of Mom's classes. We gave her a ride home once."

"She probably hasn't seen you yet," Dan said.

"I don't think she'd remember me," Ross told him. "She didn't talk to me at all. She combed her hair and talked to Mom about becoming a model."

Their pizza came, and Ross scraped off the things he didn't like and put them on Dan's plate. Their waitress was smiling at Dan each time she walked by. She was only seventeen or eighteen, Dan figured, and he kept his eyes on Ross in order to avoid meeting hers. "Why are you staring at me?" Ross said, after she took away their plates.

"Because I only get to see you once a week," Dan told him.

"It's making me nervous," Ross said.

They walked out to the car. Ross was quiet during the drive home. He was looking at the wet road ahead of them. Dan imagined Ross was thinking about the person he would become in a few years, and the girls he would meet and the places he would take them to. But a moment later it occurred to him that he could be completely wrong. He had no idea what was on his son's mind, or on anyone's, for that matter. And that realization made him feel almost stupid, and unsure of himself in a way he wasn't used to.

Later, they sat in the living room and watched a horror movie on television. Ross had put on his pajamas and was eating popcorn; when the phone rang, he didn't look up. Dan answered it in the kitchen. If it wasn't his mother with bad news about his father, he was sure it would be Robin Carter, the pretty neighbor at the horse farm who was the reason Leigh Ann had left.

"Dan?" Robin said, when he picked up the phone. "I just want to talk for a minute. I miss you."

"Ross is here," he told her. "I can't talk now. I don't have anything to say to you."

"Just say that you love me," she said, "or at least that you used to love me. Just let me hear the word."

"I can't," Dan told her.

"I'll say it to you, then," Robin said. "I love you, no matter how you feel."

"Okay," Dan said.

"Okay, like you love me back?" Robin asked.

"No," Dan said. "Just okay I heard you. I have to go." After he hung up he stayed in the kitchen for a few minutes, afraid she would call back. He sat on the floor next to Wander's blanket and watched him sleep—a big, black dog, breathing unevenly.

Dan woke up before it was light and reached out in the dark for his clothes. He dressed and walked out into the yard with Wander. It had stopped raining. The air was damp, but warm, and the sky was brightening. He ran out to the road and then up past Robin's house. Her kitchen light was on, and through the window he could see her husband standing at the sink. Her husband didn't know he and Robin had been together. Leigh Ann said, afterward, that she had known almost from the beginning. "I could tell by the way I felt about myself," she told him. "I knew you were seeing somebody prettier than I was."

He ran past the stables and down into a small valley, and then over the bridge near the few, new, isolated houses that signaled the beginning of a subdivision. Robin had talked about living with him in one of those houses. She liked the idea that everything would be modern and clean. "But they're cheaply made," Dan had told her, "so you don't get your money's worth." "I don't care," she said. "I wouldn't look at it and see below the surface, the way you would." What made Dan angry was that in spite of everything—even the fact that he didn't love her—he still wanted to see her undressed one more time. He ran two and a half miles before he turned around and came back. Robin's husband was out in the pasture, feeding his horses. He waved to Dan.

At home, Ross was in the kitchen, eating cereal. "How far did you run?" he asked his father. "I heard you leave."

"Five miles," Dan told him.

"Maybe I'll run with you next week," Ross said. "Though I'm not sure I could go that far."

"Or get up that early," Dan said. His voice was more sarcastic than he had intended, and Ross put down his spoon. Without looking at his father he carried his bowl to the sink, picked up his jacket, and walked outside. Dan stood for a minute in the center of the kitchen. Then he opened the door and walked out to the road, where Ross was standing with the dog. "Hey," he said. "You were up anyway, if you heard me leave. You were probably awake a long time before I was."

He and Ross drove back to the hospital at ten o'clock. His mother was already there. The sun had come out, and light streamed in over the foot of the bed and illuminated the wall. His father was awake, watching Ross's card trick with interest. "I could figure this out if I had the time," he told his grandson. "It's just a matter of time and concentration."

Dan took his mother down to the cafeteria for breakfast. They sat in a booth at the back of the room and watched a group of nurses at the next table pass around a wedding album. "I fell asleep in Dad's room last night, in the chair," Dan's mother told him. "I dreamed your father and I were teenagers. We were standing on a hill somewhere, looking down at a field, and I thought, I know what Andy will die of. There's something wrong with his heart. It doesn't function right, even now."

"His heart is strong, and that's what's keeping him alive," Dan said.

"You're looking at the dream too matter-of-factly," his mother told him. "I thought it was about whether or not your father loved me. Isn't that what everyone worries about?"

The cafeteria was emptying out. The nurses left, and Dan's mother picked up a newspaper one of them left behind. "I don't know what's going on in the world anymore," she said. "New York City could have disappeared and I wouldn't know about it. They could have discovered a cure for cancer." She smiled at Dan. "But then I'd know about that, wouldn't I? That would be the one thing I hope I'd know about."

They carried their trays to the conveyor belt and walked out to the elevator. Upstairs, in Dan's father's room, Ross was saying, "Let me do that trick again, Grandpa. I messed up that time. Choose a different card."

. . .

It was late on Sunday by the time Dan brought Ross back to Jefferson City. He and Ross had spent Saturday afternoon at a college basketball game in Columbia, and on Sunday they had driven to St. Louis and gone to the zoo. Ross had gotten upset in the bird pavilion, because an older man in a wheelchair had reminded him of his grandfather, but he was better after they moved on to the lion house.

Leigh Ann didn't invite Dan in. "I'm just about to take a bath," she told him. "I've been doing calisthenics for an hour. I think I could lose ten pounds if I did this every day."

"You don't need to," Dan told her.

"It would make me feel happier, though," she said.

He drove out of Jefferson City without stopping at the hospital. It was after dark. He knew his mother would still be there, and that depressed him—not because he felt sorry for her, but for a more selfish reason. He didn't want to be reminded how, unlike himself, some people were able to follow through with what they had begun years before. He almost couldn't imagine it; he felt that by turning his head away, he had given up any right to that kind of loyalty.

The moon had just come up. He noticed it as he got out of his truck, and when he went inside, he called his mother. "If Dad's awake, make sure he sees it," he said. "It's only going to look this way for a few more minutes."

Birthday

Stuart, in his old suede jacket and tennis shoes, is helping Viola into his Saab, which he left parked illegally in the alley. He received a ticket while in the process of separating Viola from her stool at the Shangri-La Tap.

"You burn me up," he tells Viola. She's in the car, leaning against the passenger door and laughing. Viola is a very small person, very thin, because she often forgets to eat. "David is mad at both of us," he says. David is Viola's son. It had been Stuart's morning to stop at Viola's, fix her breakfast, and make sure she didn't have any money for liquor. He had forgotten about the money. It was five o'clock, and she was smashed.

"Don't yell at me," Viola says. "I could be your mother."

Stuart drives her to the house he and David share. David appears at the front door in a robe, with wet hair. "We had a call from Henry," he tells Viola. Henry is the bartender at the Shangri-La. "How I love hearing from Henry."

"That sneaky creep," Viola says.

"He's the best friend you have, Mother." David helps her into the house and hands her a cup of coffee. It's David's fifty-third birthday, and in the center of the dining-room table is a whipped-cream cake with *Happy Birthday David* written on it in green icing.

Viola sees the cake and begins to cry. "I'm so sorry," she says. "On my son's birthday I have to be carted home like a runaway cat." She takes a Kleenex out of her pocket and blows her nose.

Stuart starts cooking dinner. He has all the ingredients lined up on the counter in front of his cookbooks. He's making a veal stew from a recipe he's never tried before, and he's worried that it won't come out right. He wants everything to be perfect for David's birthday, which is why he's angry with Viola. Any other day had this happened he would have had a drink with her at the Shangri-La before bringing her home, and they would have had a nice, drunken conversation. He would have done most of the talking.

"I'm running out for some wine," David says. He's dressed, holding his jacket over one shoulder, and in his hand his car keys.

"I can go in a minute," Stuart says.

"I'm all ready." David is out the door before Stuart has a chance to say anything else. For a few minutes, he stands in the center of the kitchen, then he walks over to the phone and dials a number penciled on the back page of David's address book. He hangs up before it starts to ring.

Viola is lying on the chaise lounge in the corner of the dining room; she's fallen asleep with her coat on. Stuart covers her with a blanket and removes her shoes. She smells like gin and cigarettes and another odor he's never been able to identify. Viola looks even smaller when she's sleeping, and surprisingly old. No one knows for sure just how old she is. Maybe only seventy-two, David says. Stuart stands over her and watches her breathe. He's very fond of her.

As Stuart anticipated, David is gone too long to account for a simple trip to R & B Liquors. This is part of a pattern that has been developing for months, and that, until lately, Stuart has been trying to ignore. The stew is done by the time David returns, and the three of them—Viola awake now, and fairly sober—eat in the dining room, by candlelight.

"This is fine," Viola says to Stuart. "It's very good. I should have helped you with it." She's sitting very straight in her chair; good posture is one of her favorite subjects.

"No problem," Stuart says.

Viola pushes her plate aside and lights a cigarette. "I've always loved this room," she says. It's a large room, simply and carefully lighted. David, who's an architect, designed the house inside and out.

"I wonder if you could live your whole life in a room like this if you'd turn out differently," Viola says.

"Maybe you'd just act differently," Stuart says. "Whatever happened, you wouldn't panic or go crazy."

"Even though you felt crazy," David says.

"Maybe." Stuart pulls his sweater off over his head. "The wine is good," he says evenly. "R & B Liquors?"

"No," David says. "I had to go into Hope. I wanted to get something special."

Outside, the wind is picking up and banging the atrium door that opens onto the patio. David closes it and looks out into the night—as if he can't wait to get away, Stuart thinks. He is wearing the present Stuart gave him for Christmas—a heavy cotton shirt, navy blue and a little too tight across the middle. He could be thinking anything, Stuart tells himself; he could be thinking about nothing at all.

Viola is emptying her wineglass. Stuart moves the bottle out of her reach—she's aleady had two or three glassfuls. No one has been keeping track. "I feel a thousand times better," she says. She puts her head back and exhales smoke at the ceiling. She's wearing an old-fashioned dress from the days before David's father died. She drank then, too, but for a long time no one knew. Stuart has never known a family so intent on keeping secrets.

"Let's have the cake," Stuart says. "David?"

Viola and David clear the table while Stuart makes coffee. He puts twenty candles on the cake, one for each year he and David have been together—his own secret, because David will never make the connection. It won't occur to him.

Viola is humming and stacking dishes in the sink. She stops suddenly and stands still with her wet hands held up. "A déjà vu," she says. "This has happened before. All three of us in the kitchen with the curtains open. How weird."

"Sometimes a déjà vu seems like a premonition,"

Stuart says. "You have to figure out what that one moment is supposed to mean for the future."

"Stuart is always in the dark," David says to his mother. "Life is so much simpler lived in the dark."

"That's what I like about bars," Viola says.

When Stuart has the cake ready, he and Viola sing and David blows out the candles. Viola carries her coffee and cake into the living room and turns on the television to watch the news.

David and Stuart take their cake onto the patio. All the stars are out; in the valley below, lights are shining. In a little while, Stuart guesses, David will give Viola a ride home and stay out half the night. It's an odd thing to feel powerless; it's easy, Stuart thinks. It's so much easier to be the victim. For a moment, he feels sorry for David. He knows that it causes pain to give pain, even if you believe you don't care. He, Stuart, should really fight back—this is twenty years of his life—but he would lose anyway. He has lost already. "Happy birthday," he says.

Accident

My mother's boyfriend picked me up from school the day after my friend, Jerry Weaver, was killed in a car accident east of the Superstition Mountains. It had been raining, and his car crashed through a guardrail.

I waited for Mike Russell outside, on the steps. Football practice was going on in the field next to the school, and I watched the coach running up and down, yelling. The coach was also our shop teacher. I hadn't gotten along with him since the day Jerry and I made wooden penises on the lathe. We started what was, in the coach's words, "a rash of dick making." For a few days fifteen or twenty people walked around school with wooden penises sticking out of their pants.

"Check this out," Mike said as I got into his pickup. He handed me a small, light-blue velvet box. Inside was a diamond ring. "I know the timing's bad," he said, "but I had to pick it up today, because the final install-ment was due."

"She doesn't want to get married," I said. I handed the box back to Mike. "It's nice, though," I added.

He pulled away from the curb and into the traffic. He said, "I know she doesn't, but sometimes people don't know what they want. Anyway, Brent, I'm op-timistic, and I love your mom a lot."

As I was listening to him, I was watching something happening in the other lane of traffic. "See that kid on the skateboard?" I said. "He skated right into the street without looking, and that red Mustang had to swerve to keep from hitting him."

Mike had seen it, too. He pulled the truck over and got out and walked over to the boy, who looked as though he was nine or ten. Mike, who was tall and muscular, was almost twice his size. I had my window open, but Mike was talking too quietly for me to hear him. He was motioning to the next corner, where there was a stoplight. After a few minutes he got back into the truck, and the boy skated into the street again. "Well, I really scared him," Mike said. "I told him I knew his father."

"What did he say?" I asked.

Mike started the truck. "That his father lived in Flor-ida," he said.

When we got home, my mother was sitting in a lawn chair on our concrete porch. She was still in her nurse's uniform, except for her shoes, which she had kicked off into the grass. She was the supervisor of the intensive-care unit of a hospital in Phoenix. "I think I was asleep," she said. "What time is it?"

"Four-thirty," Mike said.

I picked up her shoes and lined them up on the porch, next to the door. "Some kids didn't come to school today, Mom, because of Jerry," I said. "Tim and Danny both stayed home."

"I didn't want you here by yourself," my mother said. "I didn't want you doing nothing but thinking about it all day."

"That's what I did, anyway," I told her. "I couldn't concentrate on anything at school."

"Still, you were around other people," she said. "What are you doing?" she said to Mike, who was standing behind her chair and lifting her hair up from her shoulders.

"I'm going to rub your neck," he said.

"How come men always think they can do whatever they feel like doing?" she said. "Without even asking the other person."

"Okay, forget it," Mike said.

"I'm in a bad mood," my mother told him. "Leave me alone for a while."

Mike and I went into the house and made ourselves sandwiches. He had been going out with my mother for two years. He had a house in New River, which was twenty miles north of where we lived, but he stayed with us most of the time—he owned an auto body shop near us. Over the past two years he had taken my friends and me dirt-bike riding in the desert, and on camping trips to Saguaro Lake.

"I guess this isn't the day to give Mom the ring," I told him.

He was standing at the counter, making a cup of instant coffee. "It doesn't look like it, does it?" he said.

After I finished, I put my plate and glass in the sink

and went out the back door. Mike came out a few minutes later. I was standing next to the carport. "A Gila monster," I told him quietly, pointing to a black and yellow lizard on a rock. "I can't tell if it's dead or asleep."

"Step on it," Mike said. "That was a joke, Brent," he told me, when I didn't laugh. He stamped his foot on the ground, and we watched the lizard dart over the rock and into the carport.

"You hardly ever get to see Gila monsters," I said. "Maybe it's a sign that something else is going to happen—some other bad thing."

"Don't start thinking you can predict things," Mike said. "Don't fool yourself like that."

Next door, our neighbor came out of his house and lit his charcoal grill. He waved to us. The sun was setting and the air was suddenly cooler. There was a band of pink sky just above the desert.

"You should put on a jacket," Mike said before going into the house.

The three of us went out that night for dinner. I had wanted to stay home, but my mother said that if I didn't go, they wouldn't go. We went to a restaurant in Carefree. We hadn't made reservations and there were a lot of people ahead of us, so we sat outside on the patio. The moon was rising and the stars were beginning to appear.

Mike and my mother drank beer and I drank 7-Up. There was entertainment—a man in a Western outfit playing the piano, and an older, overweight woman in a green shimmering dress singing songs like "Frankie and Johnny." She had a green feather stole, and as she sang she wandered over to various men at the tables and draped the stole over their shoulders and sat in their laps. She brushed the stole over Mike's head on her way back to the piano, and my mother fixed his hair for him, smoothing it back from his face.

When we finally got a table, it was almost ten. We ordered dinner and my mother switched to rum and Coke. She had already had three beers. "Are you sure you want that?" Mike said when the waitress brought her the drink.

"I'm positive. I want to forget about everything," she said. She reached over and smoothed my hair in the same way she had smoothed Mike's.

"Don't," I told her.

"Okay," she said. "I'm sorry."

"I have an announcement to make," Mike said. "What the hell. I may as well do this now." He took the velvet box out of his pocket and put it on the table in front of my mother. "I bought you a ring," he said. He took it out of the box and put it on her finger. "It looks great on you, doesn't it? Like it really belongs there."

My mother looked at me and then at Mike. Her face was white. "I think I might have to vomit," she said, and put her head down on the table. After a few minutes she sat back up. "No, I'm okay," she said. "Rum always makes me sick."

Mike looked a little sick himself. He ordered tea for my mother, and when she started to take off the ring he placed his hands over hers. "I won't ask you yes or no yet," he said. "I don't want to hear no. So we'll just eat dinner and have a normal conversation. What should we talk about?"

"Let's talk about how crazy you are," my mother told him.

Our food came, and after we ate dinner Mike asked me if I'd mind if he and my mother danced. In addition to the entertainment on the patio, there was a band in the back of the room and a small dance floor. "Go ahead," I said. They got up and danced to a slow song. Afterward they came back to the table. Just as they were about to sit down, a man in a denim jacket, who was walking quickly toward the door, knocked into them and didn't apologize.

"Don't," my mother said, when she saw the expression on Mike's face. "You don't know why he did that. For all you know, he may have just found out some bad news and is hurrying home or to a hospital or someplace."

She was crying, and Mike paid the bill and we went outside and sat on the bumper of his pickup. Mike and I each had an arm around her. The moon was higher in the sky, and bright enough for me to see a glimmer of light from the ring when she lifted her hand to wipe the tears from her face. Mike was looking at the ring, too. He caught my mother's hand as she was bringing it back down into her lap. "If Jerry had been lucky," he said, "this is how the moon would have been shining on the guardrail he couldn't see."

Things to Care For

Octavia Huber was bottle-feeding her son's baby goat, which was living in a box under the skylight in her bathroom. It was six-fifteen in the morning, and it looked as if the day would be dark, and probably rainy. Right now the light leaking in was gray; it was turning the white tile and sink, and even the goat, the color of pearl. Octavia's son, Everett, who was forty-five, had been going through a bad period which was beginning to seem permanent. His wife had left him two years earlier. So, when his goat died giving birth, Octavia agreed to care for the kid until it was weaned. Everett had not felt up to it.

Octavia's daughter, Frances, called at seven. "Mother," she said, "Annette has not come home. She's out with Tom Handover, and I'm thinking of calling the police. L.G. says no. He says, 'You can't ask the police to drag your grown daughter out of her boyfriend's bed.' What do you think?"

"I think he's right," Octavia said. "And anyway, what are you doing still home?" Every Saturday, she and her daughter met at an early-morning dance-aerobics class that was held in a church basement in Monett. Frances lived farther south of that, on the other side of the Missouri state line.

"All right," Frances said. "I'm on my way, but you'll need to give me a few minutes. I'm going to drive past Tom Handover's trailer and leave Annette a note."

Octavia dressed and got into her car—a 1979 blue Ford Mustang her husband had given her new, on their thirty-fifth wedding anniversary. Her husband, a surgeon, was now married to his young reception-ist, but it was Octavia who, years before, had asked for a divorce. She had realized she'd stopped loving him.

The church that housed the aerobics class was on the corner of Fourth Street and Wren Avenue, behind a flock of sycamore trees. Octavia parked and walked into the church. The weather was humid, and hot, but the church was air-conditioned and the basement chilly. "Do some warmups, Octavia," Dorinda Lucas, the instructor, called out to her. Dorinda was sitting on the floor, next to a boom box, rummaging through a collection of tapes. She had on a black Lycra leotard and fluorescent green tights. Octavia sat down on the floor near her and did stretching exercises. She did calisthenics throughout each class; she joined the others only for the slower dance numbers.

Frances came in late, as Dorinda and seven other women were doing the Strut, to Pat Benatar. Frances waved to Octavia and took a place in the second row. "Get those feet moving," Dorinda shouted at Frances. "A healthy heart rate doesn't happen without some sweat."

"Shut your mouth," Frances said.

"Ladies, tighten up your buttocks," Dorinda yelled. "Pretend you're dancing naked past Paul Newman."

When the class was over, everyone gathered near the back wall, under the clock, and each woman took her own pulse. "It always makes me nervous to do this," Octavia said quietly, to Frances. "I don't like thinking about what's happening to my heart. I don't think it's good to be so conscious of its beating."

"Dorinda likes to do things by the book," Frances said. She and Octavia picked up their purses and left with the others. It had begun to drizzle, and they got into Frances's car and drove to a Denny's on Route 60. Frances set the climate control in her car to seventy, and adjusted her mother's seat. Frances drove a late-model Cadillac—red, with a cream interior. Her husband, L.G., was vice-president of a bank, and she had made a lot of money with a mail-order fabric business.

They sat in the last available booth at the restaurant, and each ordered eggs, grits, bacon, and coffee; Octavia substituted Egg Beaters. "As you can probably guess," Frances said, "I found Annette at Tom Handover's. I didn't need to leave a note, because there she was, at seven-thirty on a Saturday morning, cleaning out Tom's truck. This is the same girl who was too tired yesterday morning to attend her college classes. Tom was still inside, asleep. The people in the next trailer were having a yard sale. They were selling all of the garbage they hadn't bothered putting out for the trashman."

"Your idea of trash is not necessarily someone else's," Octavia said.

"Is that right?" Frances opened a container of cream and dumped it into her coffee. "What would you do with a blue statuette of a woman, minus a head? Twenty-five cents."

"I'd glue a little birdbath onto its neck and stand it in my garden," Octavia told her.

Frances looked down for a moment at her settling cream. "That's not a bad idea," she said.

After their food came, Octavia said, "Why was Annette cleaning his truck? Did you ask her?"

"I didn't have to," Frances told her. "She anticipated my question. She said, 'Mother, I'm cleaning out his truck because I want to. Last night he mentioned that it was dirty. And this morning, when I woke up early, I thought I would do this nice thing for him.' "

"Well, that was thoughtful of her," Octavia said.

"She was taking particular care with some rust spots on the inside of the door," Frances told her. "She was rubbing the edges smooth with a toothbrush." Frances ate a strip of bacon. "Probably her own."

"I seriously doubt that," Octavia said.

Frances paid for breakfast, and they walked out to the car. It was no longer drizzling; the gray sky had lightened up, and in the east, toward Branson, the Ozarks appeared to be rising out of the morning fog. Frances opened her sunroof and drove south, on Route 37, to the ranch house Everett lived in, which was set back from the highway on a big, uncared-for lawn. As Frances swung in to his driveway, Octavia noticed that his car was still up on blocks, as it had been three days earlier, when she came by in order to bring him a casserole.

"Everett hasn't been going to work," she said to Frances. Everett had inherited a concrete business that his wife's father had owned.

"I know that," Frances said. "I didn't want to tell you. I went in the other day for some paving stones."

Everett appeared, shirtless, from behind the left corner of the house. He had been letting his hair grow, and he had it pulled back with a piece of white string. He was wearing big, unlaced work boots. Octavia opened her window and smiled at him. "What do you know?" he said. He kissed Octavia and stuck his head in the car through the open window. "Man, this is nice," he told Frances. "Every time I see this car I think, L.G. knows how to live."

"I bought this car myself," Frances said. "Not that L.G. didn't offer."

"I don't think there's anything L.G. wouldn't do for you," Octavia told her.

"And I'd do anything for him, too," Frances said.

Everett opened the door for his mother and helped her out. "But the question is, Who actually paid for the car?" he said to Frances. "Behind every expensive item is a man's empty wallet."

"I paid for it, Everett," Frances said. "Get over this attitude problem. It's not becoming. It makes you sound like an asshole." She got out of the car and followed her mother and brother into the house. The living room, which Everett was using now as his workshop, was littered with screwdrivers and nails. Half of the carpeting was covered wth a large piece of plastic, and on this he had his table saw, his air compressor, and his electric drill. He was making what he referred to as "furniture for the exceptional," by which he meant tables and chairs for people of unusual size. When he had perfected his methods, he had told his mother, he planned to advertise in health-care magazines.

"Very interesting," Octavia said now, about a wobbly table tall enough to rest her chin on.

"Yes, that's fascinating," Frances told him. "No wonder you don't bother going to work anymore."

Everett went into the kitchen and returned with a plate of cookies, which he put on the table they were discussing. "I do go to work," he said. "I go when I feel I'm needed. You'd be surprised how many people aren't needed when they think they are." He and his mother and Frances jumped slightly as a mouse darted through the living room and around the corner.

"Everett, you're living with rodents," Frances said. "Set out some traps."

"Your wife's leaving you had nothing to do with need," Octavia told her son. "You're lucky she didn't need you. She'd be here for the wrong reason."

"You'd be even more miserable than you are now," Frances said. She refused the cookie Everett offered her and opened the front door. The sky had grown overcast again, and there were streaks of rain in the distance. She and her mother and Everett walked out to the small corral where Everett kept his horse, Cherry. He had bought the horse for his stepdaughter, Wendy, who was now thirteen. Wendy came back to visit only occasionally, when her mother allowed it.

"Cherry doesn't look healthy," Frances said. "What's the matter with her, Everett?"

Everett patted Cherry's nose absentmindedly. "Maybe she's lonely for Wendy, I don't know. I'll get the vet over here one of these days," he said. He looked up and squinted at a dilapidated barn a quarter of a mile away, on the property adjacent to his. "Frank Klem!" he shouted.

A tiny man in overalls, on the peak of the barn roof, raised his hand in a wave. Everett cupped his hands to his mouth. "Be careful!" he yelled. "It's very important to hold on with both hands!"

"Does Frank Klem think he can save that place?" Frances said. "He couldn't save himself in a dry bathtub." Frances had been jilted by Frank Klem in her junior year of high school.

"He takes wonderful care of his mother," Octavia said. She caught Everett and Frances exchanging a glance. "That's important when you get older," she told them. "It's something you begin to think about."

They walked around the outside of Everett's empty chicken coop, and past the pen where he had kept his goat, Dandy. "Clean up that pen for her kid, Everett," Frances said. "You need all your animals back. Some nice, new ones. You need things to care for."

"Do I?" Everett asked. He gracefully sidestepped a pile of horse manure, reached into a pocket, and brought out a handful of dried corn. "I guess I do. I still carry feed around."

"Only because he hasn't washed his pants in two years," Frances whispered to her mother, while Everett was busy picking corn and lint out of his clothes.

Octavia and Frances inspected Everett's garden—he had filled it with manure and straw, and tossed seeds into it, and, as a result, his vegetables were in no particular order—and then they walked to the car. "Thank you for coming," Everett said. "I don't get much company."

"That's something you need to remedy," Frances told him. "Clean up that junk in the living room and get out more. Go to a bar and pick up a waitress."

"It was good to see you, honey," Octavia told him. She kissed him on the cheek. "Isn't it nice that you're growing your hair! It's something a little different."

"I wouldn't encourage him in that direction," Frances told her, on the drive back to Monett.

"What direction is that, honey?" Octavia asked. Her mind was focussed on the car in front of them. An older couple was having an argument; they were waving their hands in the air, like foreigners trying to ask questions.

Back home, Octavia fed the goat, mopped the kitchen floor, and made a pot roast. She hadn't told Frances, but she had invited Annette and Tom Handover for dinner. She wanted to see what Annette had got herself into. Octavia took a bath and then she ate a sandwich in her dining room, a yellow-papered alcove with a large bay window. She looked out at the sparrows crowded around her bird feeder. The weather had not yet settled; two crows flew in under the gray sky and landed in her walnut tree, and for a few minutes big drops of rain fell on her patio. The patio was a large concrete slab Everett had poured for her one Saturday in July, three years earlier. His wife had come over with him that day, and she and Octavia had stood in the yard, watching him work. Everett's ex-wife was a small woman with long, permed hair. "Watch," she had said. "Everett's going to step back, take out a cigarette, light it, and then not smoke it," which Everett in fact had done.

"That's habit," Octavia had told her. "I'll bet you do some similar things yourself." Those are the things you love, she had wanted to add, when you love someone. Everett's wife was now living in Kansas City, with Wendy and a member of a blues band. A picture of Wendy and her mother, along with one of Everett, was still on Octavia's mantel. Octavia also had a picture of her ex-husband and his new wife. She believed that, no matter what the circumstances, life should be a process of accumulation. Life should be an effort of resistance to death, to that moment when your relatives came in and unceremoniously hauled everything away.

Annette arrived with Tom Handover at six-thirty. She was wearing a flowered dress, and she had braided a matching ribbon into her long hair. She introduced her grandmother to Tom, who was muscular and sunburned. "It's nice to meet you," he said to Octavia. He was wearing jeans and a starched white shirt. He shook her hand, and Octavia led them into the living room, where she had set out three cold beers and a plate of crackers spread with cream cheese.

"I told you she'd have beer," Annette told Tom. "Tom thought you'd have tea," she said to her grandmother. "I told him, 'No way.'" She put her hand on Tom's arm. His shirtsleeves were rolled up, and he had a tattoo on his left wrist—a dark-blue eagle with a red heart on its right wing.

"I don't need to drink beer all the time," Tom said. "Just so you don't get the wrong impression. Mostly, I have one after work."

"Tom works on a highway crew for the state," Annette explained.

"But it's not my lifelong ambition," Tom said.

"What is your lifelong ambition?" Octavia asked.

"I'm not exactly sure yet," Tom told her. "I'm leaning in the direction of heating and air-conditioning."

They finished their beers and went into the dining room, and Annette helped Octavia bring in the food. Tom stood up when they came into the room. "Oh, for goodness' sake, sit down," Annette told him. "My grandmother doesn't care about that crap."

"I do care about it," Octavia said. "It would make me sad if you brought over a man who didn't have manners, or didn't appreciate what people did for him."

"You're not referring to my last boyfriend, are you?" Annette said. "Because I know he was a huge mistake."

"No, I wasn't," Octavia told her. "Although I'm glad to hear you say that." She passed around the salad bowl and dished out the pot roast.

"That's way too much for me, Mrs. Huber," Tom said.

"You're not a vegetarian, are you?" Octavia asked. When he shook his head, she said, "I'm glad. I don't think we should just remove ourselves from the food chain. It's liable to change the balance of other things."

Tom excused himself to use the bathroom. When he returned to the table, he said to Octavia, "That's a nice goat you got there."

"Just so you know," Annette told him, "she's weaning it for my Uncle Everett."

"I think he'll be able to care for it himself in a few weeks," Octavia said.

They finished dinner as the remainder of the daylight faded outside the window. Octavia took their plates into the kitchen and returned with a cake, and after dessert they stood on the front porch and listened to the wind rustle the leaves of the maple trees that lined Octavia's walkway.

"We're in for a lot of rain tonight," Octavia told them. "I heard it forecast on the radio."

"Oh, good," Annette said. "Because what I love most is to lie in Tom's bed and hear the noise the rain makes on the roof of his trailer."

It was nearly dark. Annette kissed Octavia good-bye and drove off with Tom in his pickup. The phone was ringing as Octavia walked into the house, and she answered it. It was Frances, complaining about a note from Tom that she had discovered in one of Annette's textbooks. "No wonder she can't study," Frances said. "You wouldn't believe the things he writes to her, not to mention his spelling. I never expected to become so informed about their sex life."

"That would probably be a surprise to them, too," Octavia said. "I had Tom and Annette over for dinner tonight," she told her daughter. "I liked Tom. He's considerate and has good manners. And he cares about her. That's the important part."

"You sound just like L.G.," Frances said.

"Well, I think L.G. is right. You should look at Tom with a more open mind."

"I am open-minded," Frances said. "I haven't called the police yet."

Octavia and Frances spoke for nearly an hour. After

they hung up, Octavia went out into the back yard and sat in her lounge chair. Storm clouds were piling up in the dark sky. There were flickers of lightning within them, like flares shot up in advance of a battle. They reminded her of what Frances and Everett were doing with their lives—looking for trouble, Octavia felt, and, in Everett's case, finding it. When, in fact, they had both escaped the worst possibility in life: that of living with someone you don't love, or who doesn't love you. Outside of that, she believed, and except for death, you could conquer anything.

Venus,
Kansas

Saintly Love

Late Tuesday afternoon, Holly Parker's son, Owen, climbed to the top of the Venus water tower. There were three people in the field below—two junior high school boys playing football, and a middle-aged woman jogging—and Owen yelled down that he was going to jump.

It was the middle of September. The humid Kansas summer was finally over, and the maple trees were beginning to turn. Holly was driving to work in her Chevette, and she was angry at Owen on two counts: he had replaced Dwight Yoakum in the Chevette's tape deck with Kris Kross, and he hadn't come home after school. He was supposed to be home every day at four-thirty, before she left for work, and he'd only been managing this two or three times a week. On the other days, Holly'd learned, he hung out with dropouts in the parking lot of Wayne's Tavern, or flirted with an eighteen-year-old named Reba, or Rita, something like that, at the Tasti Freeze. Owen was just fifteen.

Will Chaffe, the owner of The Hearth, where Holly worked as a waitress, was waiting for her in the steamy kitchen; when she walked in, he sat her down in the chair under the time clock. "Owen's on top of the water tower, talking suicide nonsense," he told her. "The police are already out there, Holly." He knelt down and put his arm around her. "Now he's all right," Will said quietly. "Nothing's happened yet. Take a moment and get your breath." Holly let herself press her wet face against Will's chest, even though she knew that the cook and the other waitresses were watching her. Holly was having an affair with Will, and she was thinking, Now, in addition to everything else, they're going to know. But later, when she was able to think about it more clearly, she remembered seeing nothing on their faces but concern. The kitchen was hot and fragrant; without thinking about it, exactly, she knew that tonight's special would be fried chicken and peach cobbler.

Will suggested that one of the other waitresses, Marvelle Nest, go out to the tower with her. Marvelle was forty-eight—fifteen years older than Holly—and next to Will, she was Holly's closest friend.

"Get into my truck," Marvelle said to Holly, outside. "You can't drive and think at the same time. What I want you to think about is this. What can you say that will make Owen climb down from that tower?"

"I don't even know why he's up there," Holly said. "I don't know what's going on in his mind."

Holly put on her seatbelt, and Marvelle sped down

Oak. The water tower was east of town, past the grain elevator, out where the wheat fields began. It was five o'clock traffic, which meant a longer than usual wait at the two lights, and hesitations and false starts at the four-way stop. Marvelle drove a little blue pickup. She was a big woman with a temper, and had a reputation for barreling through town. She had a thirty-year-old son still at home, and a Vietnam vet husband, and people got out of her way.

The gravel road that circled the water tower was crowded with vehicles—the three Venus patrol cars, four state police cars, two ambulances, a fire truck, and a van that Holly recognized and had hoped not to see. It belonged to Owen's father, Burke. Holly got out of the pickup. It had been a pretty day, and now the air was cool and the wheat fields were golden in the slanting light. Marvelle held Holly's arm, and Holly looked up and saw Owen crouched like a little animal on the tiny silver platform around the perimeter of the tower.

"Tell me what to do," Holly said to Rusty Fisher, who headed the Venus police force. He was standing a little apart from the others, shading his eyes with his hand.

"The first thing is to keep a cool head," Rusty said.

Burke was walking toward them, his hands moving around in the air as though he were talking to himself. "We need that big ladder off the fire truck," he said to Rusty. "Somebody can swivel me around in that thing and I'll grab Owen." He touched Holly's hip. "Hey, honey," he said.

"I'm going to tell you this just one more time," Rusty said. "No."

"What about a trampoline?" Burke said. "How about a giant net we can catch him in? Are there any circuses around?" He walked off and grabbed the arm of a state trooper.

Rusty put his hand on Holly's shoulder. "You're shaking," he said. He went over to the police car, reached in through the open window, and came back with his jacket. He helped her on with it. He was small-boned and nice-looking. He had been Holly's boyfriend for a while in high school, but between then and now she had mostly seen him taking Burke off to jail for one thing or another. Holly and Burke were still married, though for the past year Burke had been living with a woman in the Acres of Trailers Park. Holly didn't know what to say when people, especially her mother, asked why she didn't divorce him. In spite of all the trouble Burke had caused her, Holly couldn't see bringing more pain into his life. She'd seen a lot of TV shows about women like her, and she'd come to think they had a purer kind of love than men were capable of.

A state trooper walked up to Holly. He was rugged-looking and tall, and Holly noticed that Marvelle, who was next to her, kind of came to attention. "Do you know why your son might be up there, ma'am?" he said. "Any information would help."

Holly looked down at her feet. She had forgotten, until this moment, that she was wearing her blue uniform and her white sneakers. "Well," she said slowly, "I know he doesn't come home when he should, and that he has bad eating habits. He refuses to wear clean, ironed clothes. He hardly ever talks to me, and he should brush his teeth a lot more often than he does." Holly paused, and noticed the way that Rusty and Marvelle were looking at her. She took a breath and said, "I don't have any idea why he's up there."

"You can't figure kids out anymore," Marvelle said.

The state trooper took off his hat and waved away two honey bees that were hovering around Holly's face. "What we want to do, ma'am," he said, "is have one of our people climb up there and see if we can't talk him down. We want you to tell him we won't come up all the way."

Rusty walked with her through the grass, up closer to the tower, and got her a bullhorn. The height of the tower was even more frightening to Holly up close. She could only see Owen's legs from here, dangling over the side; she couldn't see his small face or his dark hair, and she thought about how cold he must be in his thin T-shirt. "Owen," she said into the bullhorn, "one of the men here wants to climb up just a little ways, honey, so you two can talk. Raise your arm, sweetheart, if that's all right."

"Your daddy's coming up, too," Burke shouted.

"Hush up, Burke," Holly said. She watched Owen slowly raise one arm.

"All right," Rusty said. "He's giving us the go-ahead."

A state trooper with light hair took off his gun and his jacket and began to climb the tower. He moved so confidently that Holly thought, He's done this before. He saves people all the time. But then she realized how big the tower was, and how helpless he looked, climbing up. "What's he going to say to him?" she asked Rusty. "He doesn't know a thing about Owen."

"It's better that way," Rusty said. "You go up there, you and Owen are going to get into the same arguments you have at home."

"Owen!" Burke shouted. "He's not going to arrest you!"

"Shut the hell up," Rusty told him. "Damn it, Burke, you yell once more and I'll lock you up in the patrol car." Marvelle walked up behind Holly and touched her arm, and Holly began to cry.

"Doggone it," Burke said. He was wearing a big Jack Daniel's belt buckle that jabbed Holly's ribs when he wrapped his arms around her.

"Get off her," Marvelle told him. "You're no help. You're on drugs or something."

Above them, the officer had climbed to within fifteen or twenty feet of Owen. He was standing on one of the aluminum rungs, holding on in an almost casual way, Holly thought, as though he were just pausing to catch his breath and look out over the wheat fields. After fifteen minutes, the officer climbed down and walked over to Holly and the others. "Owen had a bad day at school," he said. "He failed three quizzes."

"I'll be darned," Burke said.

"What else?" Holly asked.

"There's a girl who doesn't like him," the officer told her. "And he says he's lonely. He says he wants a television and a VCR in his room."

"Jesus Christ," Marvelle said. "Why doesn't he ask for a car and a trip to Europe?"

"What do you suppose that stuff will run?" Burke said. "Can you afford it, Holly?"

Holly looked up at the tower. For one strange moment she imagined Owen falling in slow motion, in a long, lazy dive or with the fluttering motion of a leaf. But someone dropped the bullhorn, and the sound startled her into imagining Owen falling for real. "Tell him he can have both," Holly told the officer. "But only if he comes down in the next five minutes. Tell him that if he waits any longer, he'll only get the TV."

It was almost dusk. The field had become more populated; Holly saw the local TV news people, and she recognized one of her neighbors and several kids from Owen's school. In the paler light Owen looked younger and smaller to Holly, though she watched him grow steadily as he followed the officer down. The paramedics were waiting for Owen with a blanket. As soon as he stepped to the ground, they bundled him up in it.

"You had us going there for a while, son," Burke said to Owen. "You had a lot of people picturing your funeral."

"We don't need that kind of talk just now," Holly told Burke. But when he turned to look at her, she saw that he had tears in his eyes.

"Let's take a walk," Rusty said to Holly. He took her hand and led her past the cars and the tower, to the far corner of the field, where there was a creek winding through a line of cottonwood trees. It was a funny coincidence that he walked her here, Holly thought; Burke had brought her out here before they were married—if she remembered right they'd made love out here in the weeds—and he'd said he would probably shoot himself if she didn't marry him. It sounded scary to her now, but at the time Holly had thought it was romantic.

Rusty helped her across a fallen tree. "Listen," he said, "Owen will have to see doctors and such, Holly. That's the rule. And tonight he'll have to stay at the Wyatt County Hospital."

"Okay," Holly said.

Rusty shook his head. "Shit," he said. "Kids."

Holly looked at the cattails growing along the creek and at the way the wind was moving through them. The western sky was bright against the dark trees. "You should have a child yourself," Holly said. "There are some nice parts to it, Rusty. It's not mostly like this."

Marvelle and Holly followed the ambulance to the hospital. They checked Owen in, and they helped him get settled in his room. There were two beds—both empty—and Owen chose the one by the window. "I like the view," he told his mother, though when Holly looked out all she could see below were three giant dumpsters. She had bought toothpaste and a toothbrush in the hospital gift shop, along with a fishing magazine that Owen glanced at now and tossed aside. "How long do I have to stay here?" he asked Holly. "I already hate it."

"Well, it's not an amusement park," Marvelle told him. "Nobody likes it."

"Just overnight, as far as I know," Holly said. "It won't be so bad, honey. It's almost time for bed, and in the morning you'll get a good breakfast. Maybe bad nutrition was part of the problem," she told Owen. "You always eat the wrong foods, honey, and not getting enough vitamins can make you feel crazy." Holly looked out the window at the night sky. "Well, not really crazy," she said. "Just a little troubled."

Owen was lying on the bed, still dressed and wearing his shoes, flipping through the TV channels with the remote control. He turned his face away when Holly tried to kiss him good-bye.

On the way home, on the dark highway, Marvelle

drove the speed limit; Holly had noticed that Marvelle tended to do this when she was driving toward home instead of away from it.

"Do you think he'll have bad dreams?" Holly said. "I hate to think of Owen being alone and having a nightmare."

"Kids that age sleep like the dead," Marvelle told her. "Well, you know what I mean, Holly. They sleep real soundly." She unwrapped a package of gum that was on her dashboard, and offered a stick to Holly. "You don't remember the name of that big state policeman, do you?" Marvelle asked.

"Ellison, maybe," Holly said. "But I'm not sure. Maybe it was Rollison."

"I shouldn't be asking," Marvelle said. "You probably think I'm awful."

Will Chaffe had a wife and four children—though not a nice wife, Holly reminded herself—and for about the hundredth time she was tempted to confide in Marvelle about her affair. It was the only secret Holly kept from her. But when Marvelle turned on the radio and "Your Cheatin' Heart" was playing, Holly took it as a sign to keep quiet about Will. She looked out the window and said, "I don't blame anyone for going after happiness. It's just human."

At home, Holly changed into her robe and went into Owen's room, where everything was the same as always, she thought—neat, and kind of unused-looking. She wondered how she was supposed to know that Owen wanted his own TV and VCR when he hardly spent any time here. And it seemed to her that he could have just asked for them in a normal conversation, instead of climbing up a tower and telling it to the state

police. She looked at the quilt he still kept on his bed—
a brown and white patchwork, with a little cowboy in
each square. Holly knew he was going to sit on this
quilt to watch movies like *Creep Woman 2,* which would
be partly Burke's fault, she thought; when Owen was
little and his friends were watching Muppet movies,
Burke let Owen watch "Fright Theater" and the Playboy
Channel. At this moment there was a poster in the closet
that Burke had given Owen for his birthday—a nearly
naked woman on a motorcycle. Holly had already told
Owen that he couldn't put it up, but now she got the
poster out of the closet and threw it in the trash.

The phone rang, and Holly answered it in the
kitchen. "It's me," Will said. "I'll be over as soon as I
lock up." Holly listened to his voice and felt the way
she had every time she'd heard it for the past year—as
though she couldn't wait to get into bed with him. She
made herself a cup of hot chocolate and sat on her porch.
Sometime in the last hour a cold front had blown in,
and she could see pieces of the moon behind the fast-
moving clouds. Her house was at the edge of town,
across from the lumberyard. Her mother had bought it
for her, because, in her mother's words, Holly had married a loser.

A little after ten, when the phone began to ring and
kept on ringing, Holly was inside and had her television
on. She leaned forward and looked at Burke, who was
smiling for the camera, and then at her own face. She
looked so sad she almost didn't recognize herself. "Who
is that woman?" she imagined people asking. "What
kind of trouble has she gotten herself into?"

Acres of Trailers

The Hearth was not usually busy on Saturday afternoons. Most people in Venus waited until Saturday night to eat out, or went to the Porthole, Friday evening, for the catfish buffet. But this particular Saturday was an exception—maybe because it was raining and there was nothing else for anyone to do, Holly told Marvelle. The two of them, plus Will Chaffe, who was clearing tables, were handling a room full of people, many of whom were getting angry. The kitchen was backed up.

"Oh, my God," Marvelle said. She and Holly were standing at the coffee maker, and Holly watched trooper Gene Rollison walk in and sit down. He had come in only once since meeting Marvelle in September, out at the water tower. "How do I look?" Marvelle asked. "Should I take off my wedding ring?"

"He's seen you twice with it on," Holly told her,

"so you may as well not lie now." She watched Marvelle approach the table. For a big woman, Holly thought, Marvelle sometimes had small, shy ways; Holly watched her smooth down her bangs and touch the top button of her blouse before handing Gene Rollison a menu.

"Burke's getting jumpy," Will Chaffe said. He had set down a tray of dirty dishes and put his hand briefly on Holly's shoulder. "He has that look he gets before he throws things." Burke and the woman he lived with in the Acres of Trailers Park were sitting at a table beneath one of the hanging lanterns.

Holly went over and poured them more coffee. "You can see that we're busy, right, Burke?" she said. "So you can leave, or you can stay, but you can't make your food get out here any faster." She avoided looking at his girlfriend—a nineteen-year-old with long red hair and a tattoo.

"I know that, honey, but we've been waiting here a long time," Burke said. "Somebody's going to have to do something."

Holly went into the kitchen. "Cleveland," she said to the cook, "those two cheeseburgers with everything? I need them quick, before Burke goes crazy."

"Let me stab him with my butcher knife," Cleveland said.

"Okay," Holly told him, "but not until after he eats." She carried desserts out to three people, and then she put Burke and his girlfriend's food on a tray, and served it to them.

"What is this?" Burke asked.

"It's your lunch," Holly said. "You ordered it when you walked in here."

"Oh, that's right," Burke said. "It was so long ago

that I forgot." He smiled at Holly, showing the crooked front teeth that had got Holly into so much trouble sixteen years earlier, when, for reasons she couldn't remember anymore, she'd found them sexy.

Back in the kitchen, Marvelle showed Holly a slip of paper with numbers written on it. "It's Gene's phone number," she said. "He wants me to call him, Holly. What do I do?"

"Well, you make a decision," Holly told her. She felt uncomfortable giving Marvelle advice because usually, in their friendship, things went the other way around.

"I don't know if I can do that," Marvelle said. "But he's nice, Holly, I mean in addition to the other things I like about him."

Behind them, next to the deep fryer, Cleveland accidentally dropped two plates of fried shrimp. "That's it," he said. "I'm done. Tell Will I quit."

"You can't quit," Holly told him. "None of us can cook."

"The floor's clean, Cleveland," Marvelle said. "Look. Let's just brush those shrimp off and put them back on the plates. I'll give the customers free Cokes or something." She picked up the shrimp, piled them on plates, and added extra garnish.

"If Will finds out, he'll fire me," Cleveland told her.

"Who's going to tell Will?" Marvelle asked.

People were finishing up and leaving, finally, and by two-thirty the restaurant was empty. Holly stood at the front window and looked out at the rain, which had tapered off to a drizzle. The forecast was for colder temperatures and sleet, and she was already worrying; she'd told Owen he could go to a high school basketball

game that night, with a girl who had a car. If the girl
didn't take chances herself, Holly thought, Owen would
suggest them, or worse, ask to drive her car even though
he didn't have his license yet. Holly thought about how
Owen had been at the age of two, when he acted in
some of the same ways he did now, except that she could
pick him up then and put him in his playpen.

"Are they good thoughts?" Will said. He had come
up behind Holly and put his arms around her waist.
"No one's around," he told her. "Marvelle and Cleveland are in the kitchen, eating ice cream." Holly was
standing near the bulletin board Will had put up beside
the front door, with everybody's picture on it and pictures of their families. She was looking at a picture of
Will's unsmiling wife and their four young children.

"What am I doing?" Holly said, which she'd been
saying to Will for a year now.

"Making my life worth living," Will said.

At three o'clock, Holly and Marvelle changed out of their
uniforms and went grocery shopping, and then Holly
gave Marvelle a ride home. Marvelle's pickup was in
the shop; she had driven it into a barbed-wire fence two
nights earlier out of frustration with her family. "It was
dark as pitch out," Marvelle told Holly on the way home,
"and I was so fed up I just wasn't paying attention."

They were on Route 75, heading west, away from
Venus. Marvelle and her husband leased their land to
the farmer who owned the property next to theirs. Marvelle's husband, Morgan, didn't usually feel up to
working.

"It's not good for you to get so upset," Holly said. "Buy one of those self-help books. I have one that says, 'Imagine you are a river.'"

"I'm imagining something, but it's not a river," Marvelle said. She rolled down her window and then rolled it back up again. "Gene Rollison held my hand for just a minute after he paid his check," she told Holly. "And he gave me a five-dollar tip. That was more than his lunch cost."

"He's bribing you," Holly told her.

"He doesn't need to," Marvelle said. "He can probably have me for free."

Holly pulled into Marvelle's gravel driveway and helped carry in her groceries. Marvelle's ranch house was unfinished; half of it wasn't sided yet, and inside, in the kitchen and family room, the drywall wasn't sanded and you had to step over cans of paint. "We could use some help here," Marvelle said to her son, Curtis, who was sitting in a lounge chair in the family room, watching television. "There's two more bags in the back seat of Holly's car."

"I'll just wait for a commercial," Curtis said.

Marvelle made coffee, and she and Holly drank it in the kitchen. Through the rain-streaked window, Holly could see Morgan in the garage, tinkering with the motorcycle Marvelle said he'd been working on for two years. He came into the house a few minutes later. He sat down at the table, and after Marvelle poured him coffee, he put his thin hand over her large one. "I've just about got it working now," he told her. Curtis walked in with the groceries and put them on the counter.

"How are you, Curtis?" Holly asked. "What have you been doing with yourself?"

"Well, let's see," Curtis said. "Three weeks ago, I helped Harlan Reese paint his living room. Now that was a big job. And then a few months back, I delivered feed for Venus Farm Products."

"And of course he helps out around here, with this place," Morgan said.

Marvelle had her elbows on the table and her head in her hands. "Marvelle," Holly said, "did I tell you about that pretty river Owen and I saw once, on a TV special?"

"You better tell me about it now," Marvelle said.

"I believe I saw that one, too," Curtis told them. "Wasn't it in someplace like Idaho?"

Holly drove home late in the afternoon. The rain had stopped and started again, and the streetlights had come on early. She carried in her groceries and put them away, and then she went into Owen's room. He was watching music videos on his VCR. "Why don't you stay home tonight, honey?" Holly said. "The roads might be bad." She stood in the doorway and watched ten women in black garter belts dance past a rock-and-roll star.

"No way," Owen said. He looked up from his video. "I thought you wanted me to be happy."

"Well, of course I do," Holly said. "I also want you to be safe." But Owen wasn't listening anymore, and she went into the kitchen and made supper. The only things Owen would eat were white chicken meat, hamburger, and mashed potatoes, but since September, when he had been so unhappy, she had been encouraging him to eat different foods; his psychologist had suggested it. "I'd love to see Owen experiment with a healthier life-style," he had said. Tonight she made grilled fish and rice and green beans.

"Why do you want me to throw up?" Owen asked her, when he looked at his plate.

"I don't want you to throw up, Owen," Holly said. "What I want you to do is put a forkful of this food into your mouth, and swallow it."

"Well, there's no way I can do that," Owen said. He got a bag of potato chips out of the cabinet, and Holly watched him open it.

"I hope you have a child someday who's just like you," she told him.

"Me, too," Owen said.

Later, after Owen had gone out, Holly got into the bathtub and called Will at work, on her portable phone. "Are you busy?" she asked him. "Do you need me to come in?"

"Well, I need you," Will said, "but not for work. We only have five customers. Cleveland's playing solitaire. What are you doing?"

"Nothing," Holly told him. "Well, not actually nothing. I'm taking a bath."

"You're sitting in your bathtub, right now, with no clothes on?" Will asked.

"The only thing I'm wearing is soap," Holly said. "Listen." She held the phone over the water and sloshed the water around.

"Oh, my," Will said. "Oh, my, my."

"You already said that," Holly told him.

"Did I?" Will said. "Am I repeating myself? Should I stop by after I close up, and see if I can't talk any straighter?"

"I wish you could stop by right now," Holly told him, "but later isn't going to work, because Owen could be back any time."

"Shoot," Will said. "Well, I suppose I should get home, anyway. Not that I want to, Holly. You know that."

Holly held the phone tightly to her ear. "Will," she said, "tell me the truth now. Do you really love me?"

"More than anything," he said.

After Holly got out of the bathtub and was sitting in her robe, in the kitchen, wondering if Will would kiss his wife when he got home, and if he'd get any pleasure from it, Marvelle's face appeared at the kitchen door. Holly let her in, and Marvelle took off her raincoat and shook it out.

"I took Morgan's Jeep," she told Holly. "He was out in the garage, and Curtis was lying on the couch, watching a movie about rabbit robots. I couldn't stand it anymore. Also, I couldn't stop thinking about Gene Rollison."

"Thoughts like that can get you in trouble," Holly said.

"I don't care," Marvelle told her. "I need some different troubles from the ones I have." She sat down across from Holly. "Anyway, I think I'm in love with Gene."

"You've hardly even talked to him," Holly said.

"I know," Marvelle told her. "Can you imagine how I'm going to feel when I know him better?" Holly watched her stand up and walk over to the window. "I feel restless," Marvelle said. "Put on some clothes and let's go for a drive somewhere."

"It's raining," Holly said. "The roads are supposed to get bad."

"The roads are fine. You need to get out more, Holly. You can't sit home all the time just because it's safe. You should take a risk now and then."

"I do take risks," Holly said, and she went into the bedroom, just then, to get dressed, so that she wouldn't talk too much and tell Marvelle about Will. She and Marvelle ran outside through the rain and got into the Jeep. Marvelle drove around town, past The Hearth and the supermarket and the hardware store, and then out to the Stop Time. She pulled up next to the phone booth.

"I'm going to call him," she told Holly. "I've been wanting to do it all night—dial his number and hear him answer. It makes my heart beat fast just thinking about it."

Holly stayed in the Jeep and listened to the radio. The third song to come on was Patsy Cline singing, "Crazy." It was Holly's favorite; she believed it described herself, in the relationships she'd had. She thought that love, in general, made people act insane.

"I've never done anything like this before," Marvelle said, when she got back in the Jeep. "Well, almost never. I kissed that trucker once. Do you remember him, Holly? He used to come into The Hearth. Bob something-or-other."

"Bob Sanders," Holly said. "He's a friend of Will's."

"How do you know that?" Marvelle asked.

"Oh," Holly said. "I don't know. I heard it from somebody."

Marvelle started the Jeep, but a moment later she

put her head down on the steering wheel. "My God, Holly," she said, after she sat up, "there I was, listening to his deep voice, and I imagined I had my hands on his chest, and it was all I could do not to tell him I wanted to come over and unbutton his shirt." She put the Jeep into gear and pulled out onto the highway. "But I didn't say anything like that. Instead, I told him about my carrot crop last spring. Don't ask me why."

The rain on the canvas roof was steady and loud; it reminded Holly of the camping trips that she and Burke used to take, when Owen was little. "Did you know that Burke was a Boy Scout?" she said to Marvelle. "He earned camping badges and everything."

"Is that right?" Marvelle said.

"I think that was where he was meant to live," Holly told her, "out in the wilderness someplace, where there aren't any people to get on his nerves." She noticed that Marvelle had both hands on the steering wheel. "The roads are getting slippery, aren't they?" Holly said. "And here we are, running all over town. I hope Owen is all right."

"You worry about him too much," Marvelle told her.

"I know," Holly said. "I worry about everything too much." They were on the south side of Venus, near the Acres of Trailers Park, and Holly thought about how, if she'd been alone, she'd have driven through the park and looked for Burke's van so that she would know he was all right—even though she knew he was probably in bed, holding his girlfriend in his arms.

"I'm so tired," Marvelle said. "There are all those talk shows about people having affairs. How come no one talks about how tired it makes you?"

"You haven't had an affair," Holly said.

"Well, I feel like I have," Marvelle told her. "I feel like I've been to the waterbed and back." She pulled up in front of Holly's house, which was brightly lit. "See?" she said. "Owen's fine. Nobody you care for is dead, or lying in a ditch, or sick in a hospital."

"Nobody that I know about, anyway," Holly said. She told Marvelle good night and went inside. Owen was asleep, and there was a note from him on the kitchen table that said, "Where the hell are you, Mom?" Holly decided to save it for her scrapbook, since it was the nearest thing to affection that she could probably hope for from Owen.

In bed, in the dark, she listened to the house creak. Her house was old, and it had about fifty things wrong with it. Will's house was a new split-level in a subdivision; Holly had only been inside once, a few weeks earlier, when his wife had taken the kids to Topeka, and neither she nor Will had been able to make love there. It wasn't just because it was where his family lived, Holly thought, but because the house was too perfect. It didn't have imperfections and problems. It wasn't temperamental: it didn't give you a nervous stomach or keep you up at night. She and Will had driven out into the country, that day, in her old car, and made love in the back seat among a bunch of comic books and an abandoned shoe and a lot of other things—things somebody will love you for, Holly thought, if you're lucky enough to be loved.

Dreams

Morgan Nest had a heart attack Saturday morning as he was standing in his driveway, working on his motorcycle. Holly didn't find out about it until late the next afternoon. She had gone to Kansas City for the weekend with Will Chaffe. "I called and called," Marvelle told her. "Finally I called Burke and talked to Owen, and Owen said, 'Mom went shopping in Kansas City.' But I didn't think you'd stay there the whole weekend by yourself, Holly."

They were sitting in a small waiting area near the elevators on the fourth floor of the Wyatt County Hospital. Holly looked at her friend's face and felt terrible about lying. There were circles under Marvelle's dark eyes, and her face was pale. Marvelle and Curtis had spent the night at the hospital, sleeping on the sofa.

Now Curtis had gone home to feed his father's hunt-

ing dogs, and Holly and Marvelle had the waiting area
to themselves. They were sitting in orange vinyl chairs
next to a window; Holly could see the hospital parking
lot below, and beyond that, an open field. It was early
March. The air was still cold, but the snow they'd had
a week earlier had melted. Even now Holly could see a
flock of birds in the distance—geese, maybe, she
thought. The sun had not gone down yet, as it would
have a month earlier at this time.

"I saw it happen," Marvelle said. "I had baked a pie,
which was in the oven, I was thinking about frying a
chicken for lunch, I was thinking about throwing a shoe
through the TV, because Curtis was watching it twenty-
four hours a day, as usual, and I looked out the window
and saw Morgan put down the motorcycle part he was
holding. I watched him fall." Marvelle got a Kleenex
out of her pocket. "It was like somebody hit the back
of his knees."

Holly put her arms around Marvelle. "Morgan will
be all right," she said.

"How do you know?" Marvelle asked her.

"It's a feeling I get. I can tell sometimes how things
will turn out." This was Holly's second lie—she felt
that she could never tell how anything would turn out—
but she had just read an article in the car, as she and Will
were driving back to Venus, about how happiness was
connected to being optimistic. "He's going to be completely okay," Holly said. "But I'm worried about you.
How long has it been since you've eaten?"

"I don't know," Marvelle said. "Maybe yesterday."

Holly went down to the cafeteria and brought back
sandwiches and coffee for both of them, and then she
called Burke from the pay phone in the hall to ask if he

could bring Owen home at ten, instead of keeping him all night. She hated to think of Owen sleeping over again in that trailer with Burke and Burke's nineteen-year-old girlfriend. Owen was sixteen, and one weekend the girlfriend had fixed him up with her twin sister.

As she spoke to Burke, Holly could see Marvelle down the hall, standing in the doorway to Morgan's room. Marvelle looked almost fragile now to Holly because her jeans and shirt were too big for her. Lately, Marvelle had been wearing tighter clothes when she came into town, in the hope, Holly knew, of running into Gene Rollison.

"Burke," Holly said for the third time, in an effort to interrupt a long story he was telling about how he got screwed out of money by three people. "Just tell me yes or no. I have to get off the phone."

"Yes," Burke said.

"Okay. And make sure he does his homework," Holly told him. "Don't let Owen tell you he doesn't have any, or anything like that." Burke was quiet, and after a moment Holly said, "I'm sorry those things happened to you, Burke. Really. I can see how you were just the innocent victim."

"That's exactly right," Burke said.

Holly got off the phone and walked up to Marvelle, who whispered, "You wouldn't believe how different Morgan used to look, Holly, back before Vietnam." Holly had been just a child during the war—Morgan was the only person she knew who'd actually been there. But she'd seen pictures of Marvelle's wedding, which had taken place in 1962, years before Morgan was drafted, and in the pictures Morgan looked young and happy. In the six years Holly had known Morgan, she'd never seen him look happy.

"Let's go for a walk," Holly said. "You can't make him get better by watching him." She got Marvelle's coat—an old gray canvas duster that Curtis had probably worn back in high school—and they went down in the elevator and outside through the big automatic doors. Holly stood on the steps for a minute and breathed the cool air. Hospitals frightened her. She couldn't walk down the halls without imagining what each sick person was thinking and feeling. She knew that in her mind she turned them all into better people than they probably were; for all she knew, the elderly man in the bed next to Morgan had murdered his wife or had tortured children, but Holly couldn't get past the fact that no matter what, he—and all the other patients—were helpless now. All that helplessness made her feel like she was drowning.

She and Marvelle walked away from the hospital in the direction of the setting sun. They ducked under a fence and walked through the field Holly had seen from the fourth floor. "When Morgan's better," Holly said, "he can sit next to the window and watch for deer."

"And smoke cigarettes, if it were allowed," Marvelle said. "That's what he'll want to do, Holly. He'll go right back to smoking himself to death and drive me crazy."

The other side of the field was bordered by a row of trees, and they walked beyond that to the edge of a pond. This was probably where the geese were headed to, Holly thought, or leaving from, but now there weren't any birds at all. There wasn't even a ripple on the water. There was only the faint rustle of something alive in the long grass. A whole world full of animals and insects probably lived here, Holly was thinking, but then she stopped herself before she started to worry about them the way that she was worrying about the strangers in the hospital. "Did you get anything nice in Kansas City?" Marvelle said. "I forgot to ask you that."

"The shopping wasn't that good," Holly told her, although the truth was that she and Will had spent almost the entire weekend in a king-size bed. They'd only left the room to eat in the hotel restaurant, and to buy toys for Will's children. Watching Will choose the toys had made Holly feel angry at first, and then selfish, and finally just sad. It made her realize how much she had managed to pretend that he wasn't married. Holly's own marriage, because Burke was living in another place, with another woman, hardly counted, Holly thought. It was just a technicality.

"Let's you and me go to the mall in Lawrence sometime, if Morgan gets better," Marvelle said. "I'll buy presents for everyone I know." She and Holly walked back through the field. It was almost dark by the time they got to the hospital, and they stood for a minute in the bright lobby and let their eyes adjust to the light.

"Mom," Curtis said. He startled them both, walking up behind them in his rubber boots. He said hello to Holly, and then sank down on a yellow couch. "Somebody called you," he told his mother. "Some state trooper. He wanted to know how Dad was."

"I see," Marvelle said. Holly watched her take a deep breath. "Well, that's a man Holly and I know, honey. He comes into the restaurant, and I bet that's how he knows about Dad, since he's friends with all of us at

The Hearth. I bet Will Chaffe or somebody told him."

"Well, whoever he is, he called." Curtis yawned and stretched out his big legs. Holly watched him. Whenever she wanted to give herself a scare, she pictured Owen still living at home with her when he was thirty.

"Curtis, will you go upstairs and check on your dad?" Marvelle asked. "Holly and I'll just visit the rest room and get some Cokes."

"I don't want to do it right now," Curtis told her. "I'm tired from feeding all those dogs."

Marvelle and Holly went up in the elevator. "Has dog food gotten heavier since I had a pet?" Holly asked.

"What?" Marvelle said. "Oh. Curtis has a weak back." She and Holly got off the elevator, and Marvelle stopped suddenly in the middle of the hall. "What does Gene expect me to do," she said, "come running over to his house even though my husband is half dead? Does he think I still feel the same way about him now that this has happened?"

"Why wouldn't you?" Holly said.

"I wish I'd never met him," Marvelle told her. "He was a big mistake in my life. He's probably the reason Morgan had a heart attack. Anyway, Holly, I never even kissed Gene. I wanted to, but the day he and I were finally someplace private, I remembered that I forgot to brush my teeth." She and Holly peeked into Morgan's room, to make sure he was still asleep. "Although I did hug him a lot," Marvelle whispered, out in the hallway. Holly followed her to the rest room, and then back down the hall to the waiting area where Curtis was sitting now, reading a magazine about big trucks. She and Marvelle sat down across from him.

"Truck driving would be a good profession for

you," Holly said after a few minutes. "It would get you out of Venus."

"I like Venus," Curtis said.

"You could go anywhere you wanted, though," Holly told him. "You're still young, and you don't have a family to take care of."

"Who do you think is sick in that bed down the hall?" Curtis said.

"Don't be snotty," Marvelle told him. "You know what Holly means, honey. It's not like you're supporting us."

"That's right," Holly said. "In fact . . ."

"In fact," Marvelle interrupted, "I think you would be happier if you didn't have Dad and me to worry about."

Holly walked down the hall to get a drink of water so that she could be away from Curtis for a few minutes. It was only eight-thirty, but most of the patients in the rooms were asleep. She felt sad, thinking about their dreams. Even if they were sweet ones, she thought, the patients would have to wake from them in the morning and find themselves trapped in hospital beds. It reminded her of birds that flew into what looked like space but turned out to be glass. For the third time that evening, Holly found herself on the verge of tears. She wanted to think that she was crying for the patients, or for Marvelle's sake, but she felt instead that she was crying over the affair she was having with Will.

"Did you ever notice how one sad thing will remind you of other sad things?" she asked Marvelle a few minutes later, as the two of them were looking at recipes in a magazine. Curtis had gone downstairs to the cafeteria.

"What things are you being reminded of?" Marvelle said.

"Well, like how you can love someone much more than you should," Holly said, "and what it would be like not to have anyone love you."

"It would be lonely," Marvelle told her.

"And also really sad," Holly said. Curtis got off the elevator, carrying a deck of cards, and Holly and Marvelle cleared off the magazine table and played hearts with him. He won often enough for Holly to be fairly sure he was cheating. "Are you always this lucky?" she asked him.

"You wouldn't believe it, Holly," Marvelle said. "It's like the perfect cards just appear in his hand."

Holly left a little before ten. She said good-bye to Curtis and walked down the hall with Marvelle, to look in one more time on Morgan. "He looks better already, don't you think?" Holly whispered. "He looks almost recovered." She told Marvelle she'd come back to the hospital in the morning.

Outside, it felt like winter again. As she got in her car, she tried to remember what the weather had been like in Kansas City. She could only recall sitting up in bed, once, and hearing what sounded like either wind or rain. "What difference does it make what it's like out?" Will had asked her. But Holly thought it was scary to lose track so much of what was really happening.

At home, Owen was sitting on his bed, watching television. "I had Dad bring me home early," he told Holly. "I was ready to get out of there. They made me go bowling last night."

"What's wrong with bowling?" Holly asked.

"It's what geeks do," Owen said. "Geeks and fat people."

Holly hung up his jacket, wondering what made her miss Owen when she was away from him. The idea of Owen, she thought, was nicer than Owen, himself. "Tell me a good thing that happened this weekend," she said.

"Okay." Owen rolled up his sleeve and showed Holly that he'd had his initials tattooed on his forearm.

"Jesus Christ," Holly said. "This was your father's idea, wasn't it?"

"No," Owen said. "The tattoo guy thought of it."

Holly was too tired to call Burke and yell at him. She told Owen to go to sleep, and then she lay down on her bed in her clothes, with the light on. She didn't wake up until 8:30 A.M., when the phone rang and Marvelle said, "Morgan will probably be all right, Holly. The doctor just told me."

Owen was half asleep. He had missed his bus, and his first class was half over. Holly sat on the edge of his bed in her wrinkled clothes. "Owen," she said, "neither of us set the clock."

He opened his eyes. In the morning, Holly thought, before he was awake enough to put that sarcastic expression on his face, he still looked like a small boy. Without thinking, she put her arms around him the way she used to, when he was small enough to carry.

"What's wrong with you?" he said.

"Nothing, honey. I heard that Morgan will be all right." Holly was already drawing back from him, but to her surprise Owen hadn't moved. He put his arms

176

around her for just a second—just long enough for Holly to know that he was actually touching her—and then he sat up and yawned. "It's cool, isn't it?" he said, when he noticed her looking at his tattoo. "I'd get another one except the needle creeped me out."

"I'm not going to see Gene Rollison anymore," Marvelle told Holly at ten-thirty, as the two of them were sitting in the hospital cafeteria, eating breakfast. "He's a good person and everything, but look at what almost happened to Morgan."

"That had nothing to do with Gene," Holly said.

"How do you know it didn't? Anyway, I can't have all these emotions. I only want to have one feeling at a time."

"Like unhappiness?" Holly said.

"That's right," Marvelle told her. "That's enough for me."

Holly left the hospital at noon. She planned to drive to The Hearth to see Will, even though she would see him that night when she went in for work. All the time they had spent together in Kansas City had made her even lonelier for him. But as she got close to the restaurant she had an uneasy feeling. It wasn't guilt, she knew, like Marvelle's decision not to see Gene, which Holly figured would disappear the minute Morgan was back on his feet. It was something more serious than that. It was like the thing about the bird and the window. She and Will were dreaming, or at least she was, and if she was going to smash into something, she wanted to know beforehand. She wanted to be awake, at least.

Holly drove slowly past The Hearth. The day was cloudy, and through the window she saw that the red lanterns were turned on; she could see the bright table-cloths and the stiff-backed chairs. She could even see Will, standing at the counter, and she allowed herself to imagine for just one heartbroken moment how he would feel watching her drive by. But she kept on going.

ABOUT THE AUTHOR

Judy Troy has taught creative writing at Indiana University and the University of Missouri–Columbia, and is currently at Auburn University in Auburn, Alabama. She is fiction editor for *Crazy Horse,* the literary review of the University of Arkansas at Little Rock. She was awarded the Eban Demarest grant, and her work has appeared in *The New Yorker, Icarus, Witness,* and *Antaeus,* as well as in the anthology *Growing Up Female: Short Stories from the American Mosaic.*